Murder Under the Mistletoe

A BITE-SIZED BAKERY COZY MYSTERY BOOK 5

ROSIE A. POINT

Murder Under the Mistletoe

A Bite-sized Bakery Cozy Mystery Book 5

You're invited!

Hi there, reader!

I'd like to formally invite you to join my awesome community of readers. We love to chat about cozy mysteries, cooking, and pets.

It's super fun because I get to share chapters from yet-to-be-released books, fun recipes, pictures, and do giveaways with the people who enjoy my stories the most.

So whether you're a new reader or you've been enjoying my stories for a while, you can catch up with other like-minded readers, and get lots of cool content by visiting my website at *www.rosiepointbooks.com* and signing up for my mailing list.

Or simply search for me on *www.bookbub.com* and follow me there.

I look forward to getting to know you better.

Let's get into the story!

Yours,
Rosie

One

If there was one thing I wanted to avoid this holiday season, it was murder.

Well, surely everyone wanted to avoid murder in general, but after the past few months Bee and I had had on the Bite-sized Bakery food truck, it was a valid wish.

Since we'd arrived in Carmel Springs, Maine, we'd investigated not one, not two, but a total of four murders! Some of the investigations had been out of necessity and others because we'd fallen into the trap of wanting to know more.

Curiosity killed the cat. So far, the satisfaction hadn't brought anything but the icy weather.

Bee hummed under her breath on the truck beside me, wearing a Santa Claus hat with a bell on the end. It was our last day on the truck for the year, but only because there was a Northeaster on the way, and the locals had warned us that staying out here was more than foolish. Potentially life-threatening.

"Can you believe Christmas is only a few weeks away?" Bee asked as she prepared us each a cup of scalding hot coffee. "The year has flown. Thanksgiving is over. We've gotten to know everyone in this town, and I just can't..."

"What?"

"Nothing. I just realized what I what I sounded like," Bee said, showing me her signature gap-toothed grin. "I'm not an emotional person. It seems like Carmel Springs has softened me up. There must be something in the water."

"Or the lobster."

"Or that," she said and rubbed her gloved hands together. "Good heavens, it's like the air is ice out here."

"Do you want to call it a day?"

"We haven't even had our first customer yet, Rubes," she replied. "Are you all right? Feeling ill?"

"I'm fine. Just not used to the cold." And I had a strange feeling in the pit of my stomach that something was bound to go wrong soon. We'd had lovely peace and quiet ever since Thanksgiving. There had been no murders, crimes or investigations.

As much as I loved investigating them—that came

with the territory after having been an investigative jour-nalist—I would definitely have preferred that no one in town was harmed.

"Are you sure you're OK?" Bee asked, narrowing one hazel eye at me.

"I've got the tingles," I said.

"Hmm. Care to elaborate?"

"The investigative tingles."

"Meaning what?"

"That I feel like something's on the horizon. Some-thing big."

"Well," Bee said, "that's because there is something big on the horizon, Rubes." She paused for effect, spreading her hands. "Christmas! And our Christmas party. As for anything else, I think the lack of sun is getting to you."

She was right about that. The sky was a dull gray, and the ocean was dark, the beach empty. The hours had grown longer as we approached the thick of winter. Maybe my apprehension was more to do with that and having to leave the wonderful Oceanside Guesthouse that we'd called home for so long.

The folks here had finally accepted us, and now we were going to leave on our next great baking adventure.

"Good morning." Millie's warm greeting cut across my negative thoughts. She pottered into view, wearing a thick coat and a pair of matching woolen gloves. "You two are brave coming out here. I don't think you'll be getting many customers on a morning like this. Ice in the air, ice in the veins."

"Agree," I said. "I was just thinking we should call it a morning."

"Mind if I get one of your candy cane cupcakes and a cup of hot coffee before you do?" Millie asked, removing the newspaper from under her arm.

"Coming right up," Bee said and set to work getting Millie's order together.

"Is that the newest issue of the paper?" I asked.

Millie waved the local paper around then slapped it down on the food truck's side counter. "That's right. This one's great. My writers worked extra hard, and I appreciate that, given that it's Christmastime. It sure makes my job easier." As the editor of the newspaper, Millie had her ear to the ground at all times. She was a great friend and resource.

Listen to me. I can't stop thinking in investigative terms. Good heavens, it's Christmas. I need to relax.

"Anything interesting happening for Christmas?" I asked.

"Oh, well, let me see," Millie said, opening the newspaper and laying it flat. The scents of roasted coffee drifted through the air, mingling with the cold bite of salt off the ocean. "There's the local carolers group looking for new members."

"Hard pass," Bee said. "In this weather? They must have a death wish."

"Ooh, don't say that." I grimaced.

Bee rolled her eyes at me.

"Let's see, what else. Ah yes," Millie said, fumbling to turn pages with her gloved fingers. "Mayor Jacobsen was recently re-elected."

"He was?"

"Yes, in November. Hotly contested too. It was the first time in years he had a competitor for the post," Millie said, "and that made things interesting and fun too. He actually looked nervous about finding out the results. So, he's having somewhat of a celebration for it. Though I don't know if you could call the Christmas tree lighting a celebration."

"Oh, I heard about that," I said. "They're doing that tomorrow night."

"Yeah," Millie replied. "Everyone's going to be there. Though I think most of them are going to see if anything happens."

"What do you mean?" Bee handed over the candy cane cupcake and cup.

Millie took a sip of coffee and smacked her lips. "Well, everyone's heard that the Babcock's on the prowl."

"I'm sorry, the...?"

"The Babcock," Millie said, somewhat mysteriously, with a wriggle of her silver eyebrows.

"Is that some type of mythical creature native to Maine?" Bee asked.

"Oh, no, no. Everyone knows that if there was a mythical creature, it would be a lobster-eating sea monster, not a land-dwelling creature," Millie replied and took a bite of her cupcake. She chewed slowly, clearly enjoying the growing suspense.

"Who is the Babcock?" I asked.

"Or what?"

"It's a 'who,'" Millie replied. "A 'him' to be more specific. He's the local butcher, Clayton Babcock. Everyone calls him 'the Babcock' because he's such a force to be reckoned with. And he thought he was too when he went up against Jacobsen for the position of mayor. But he didn't win."

"What's any of this got to do with the lighting of the Christmas tree?" Bee's brow wrinkled.

"Apparently, the Babcock is furious that he didn't get elected. He believes that there was some fiddling with the votes," Millie continued, "which is patent nonsense, of course. Everyone knows that the votes are counted electronically. We had a new system installed last year, on Mayor Jacobsen's urging."

Millie took another bite of her cupcake and chewed. "The Babcock," she said, "threatened to chop down the Christmas tree because of his displeasure. The man really believes that laws don't apply to him. I have it on good authority that a few police officers had to attend to a disturbance at the butcher's shop a few days ago because he was making so much noise about it."

"Do you think he'll do something like that?" Bee asked. "Chop down the tree?"

"No one knows," Millie said. "But if he does, you can bet your bottom dollar I'm going to be there to see it."

"Count us in." Bee clapped her hands together. "Ruby needs something to cheer her up."

"Oh no. Why? What's wrong?"

I shook my head. "Nothing. I've just got the strangest feeling that something's going to go wrong. Maybe I'm being paranoid."

"Or you're predicting the untimely demise of the Christmas tree tomorrow night," Millie said, her sharp blue eyes glimmering. "I'll see you then, ladies." She waved goodbye and carried her cupcake and coffee back to her car. She left behind the newspaper.

I picked it up. The black and white picture of the decorated Christmas tree was front and center, Mayor Jacobsen standing next to it, grinning from ear-to-ear, his belly straining against a smart black coat. "Come on, Bee. Let's close up and go have a cup of cocoa."

"I thought you'd never ask."

"I didn't ask," I said, quizzically.

"Oh, you know what I mean." Bee whistled as she helped close up the truck, infected by the Christmas spirit. I wished I could've felt the same.

Two

The evening of the tree lighting had
arrived, and we gathered in front of the town hall, shoulder-to-shoulder. I hugged my coat to my chest and rubbed my gloved hands over my arms. It was cold as could be, and the breaths misted in front of the faces of the crowd members.

Practically everyone in Carmel Springs had turned out for the event and had gathered in front of a raised podium. Behind it, shrouded in darkness by the clouded sky, sat the shadowy shape of the Christmas tree.

"What time is it supposed to start?" Bee asked, her teeth chattering.

Sam, the owner of the Oceanside Guesthouse, brought her phone out and checked the time. "It was due to start over a half an hour ago. I wonder what's going on."

The light from the lamps on the other side of the street provided some illumination, but the area in front of the town hall had been left mostly in darkness, so the lighting would draw the maximum amount of oohs and ahs from the crowd.

I stamped my feet in my ankle boots and peered around. All the usual "suspects" had turned up to witness the lighting of the Christmas tree—holiday celebrations were an important part of life in Carmel Springs.

There was Millie, the editor of the local paper, her gray hair pulled up into a bun and her cheeks pink from the cold. Ava, Mayor Jacobsen's wife, stood closer to the front, occasionally frowning and checking her phone. Benjamin Pelletier, the owner of the Lobster Shack, paunchy, tan and graying, kept making loud remarks about how late it was getting.

"C'mon, hurry it up. It's freezin' out here," he called.

Seeing him reminded me of Owen, his nephew, who'd lost his life just months ago. Poor Owen—he'd had his problems, as far as our investigation had discovered, but no one deserved death by lobster mallet.

Goodness, it was so strange—I'd gotten to know the people in this town over the past few months. I was more at home in Carmel Springs than I'd been in New York, for heaven's sake. These people were friends and family to me. Sam in particular.

I rubbed my gloves together again. "Now I'm not usually one to side with Benjamin Pelletier," I said, "but he's got a point. It's freezing."

"And getting late," Bee put in.

"Maybe we should find out what's going on from Ava?" Sam gestured to the mayor's wife.

The woman, who had blonde, wispy hair tied back in a low ponytail, appeared glued to her phone. Not even a tap on the shoulder seemed likely to disturb her. Folks these days were obsessed with technology.

A smattering of applause rang out as a figure proceeded to the podium carrying an old-timey lantern, flame steady. He placed it on the wooden lectern's surface and light spilled over his face. Immediately, the gossiping and whispering began.

It wasn't Mayor Jacobsen.

It was another man—one I didn't recognize. He was handsome and young, with thick, curly ginger hair and a broad smile. His eyes were quite far apart and sparkled by the light of his lantern. "Settle down, settle down," he said, patting the air.

"Who's that?" I whispered.

Sam opened her mouth to answer, but the new guy patted the microphone, and it let out a horrendous squeal. Everyone yelped or groaned.

"Some of you know me already, but for those of you who don't, the name's Babcock. Clayton Babcock."

"That' the Babcock Millie was telling us about?" I asked.

"Seems like it," Bee replied. "Heavens, I was expecting someone of mythical proportions. Like Goliath."

A few hisses sounded behind us as people listened in on what this Babcock guy had to say. Odd, really, that he was here after Millie had told us he might ruin the celebration out of jealousy.

"Now, I know you're all excited to get this tree lighting underway," the Babcock said, that grin hardly shifting. It was remarkable he could get the words out past those sparkling white teeth. "And y'all have been very patient already. But here's the thing. Mayor Jacobsen isn't here yet."

Another round of groans and griping started up.

"I can't stand here another minute," Benjamin shouted. "It's too cold. I'm freezing my toes off."

"Don't worry about it," the Babcock said, with another winning grin. "I'm here to do the tree-lighting ceremony myself."

"But he's not the mayor," Sam whispered. "Where's the mayor?"

"Unfortunately, we can't wait any longer." Babcock spread his arms, as if to welcome us all to his party. "So, let's get this started. I wanted to thank you all for being here today. Christmas is a special time for most families, and in Carmel Springs, that's especially true. We're a community, and Christmas is to be celebrated and enjoyed with each other."

The crowd had fallen silent again but folks stamped their feet and rubbed their arms. I joined in. It seemed as if this Mr. Babcock liked the sound of his own voice.

"If the carolers would step up, please," Babcock said, gesturing to the bleachers that had been erected next to his podium.

The caroling choir took their positions, most of them with festive scarves wrapped around their necks.

"And now, it's my great pleasure to light the Carmel Springs Christmas tree!" Babcock hit a switch on the lectern.

The choir took up "Away in a Manger." Strings of lights flickered on in the magnificent Christmas tree, all in shades of whites and reds and blues, greens and yellows and—

A scream cut through the noise.

One of the carolers, standing on the uppermost tier of the bleachers, slapped her hands to her cheeks. She shook her head, wide-eyed, staring at the Christmas tree. She screamed a second time and then a third, and I turned, searching for what had spooked her.

"Oh no," I whispered. "Not again."

Right there, tucked away under the Christmas tree, lay Mayor Jacobsen, his eyes wide and staring and a string of lights wrapped around his neck.

"What's going on?" Sam asked, rising up on tiptoe as more screams broke out. "Is everything—?" Sam spotted the mayor's body and screeched.

"Don't look," I said.

Panic took hold in the crowd—people yelled, pushed, ran this way and that, and a stampede started. I grabbed Sam and Bee's arms, and we formed a chain, hurrying backward and away from the struggle.

"This is terrible," Sam said. "The poor mayor."

Bee nodded, pale in the face. "I wonder who did it."

Three

Nothing dampened the Christmas spirit quite like murder. The crowds had continued screeching and freaking out right up until the police had rolled up in their cruisers. Everyone had been separated, and the scene had been cordoned off.

There were too many suspects to interview at once, so the officers had taken everyone's names for later follow-ups. Sam, Bee, and I stomped up the front steps of the Oceanside Guesthouse in silence, the icy temperature frosting our breaths.

Sam unlocked, and we bundled into the warm entry hall, shutting the door behind us.

"Terrible," Sam said, faintly, as she stripped off her gloves. "Just terrible. I can't believe poor Mayor Jacobsen is dead."

"And in such a horrible way, too."

We hadn't known Mayor Jacobsen all that well, but it was upsetting to think that it had happened to him. He'd come over to the guesthouse around Halloween and had been complimentary to Sam on her food and decorations. He'd seemed a nice enough guy. And now, he was gone.

"Another murder in Carmel Springs," Bee said, shaking her head.

"Who would do something like this?" Sam asked. "I don't understand why anyone would hurt the mayor. He was a good man."

Meow! Trouble the cat pattered out of the living room and rubbed his furry calico face against Sam's legs. He came over to me next, and I bent and scratched behind his ears.

"Hello, sweetheart," I said. "It's good to see you again."

"I need a strong cup of coffee." Sam shrugged off her coat and hung it up on the rack. "I bet Frank will be over here soon."

"Frank?" I asked.

"Oh." Sam's cheeks colored pink. "Detective Martin, I mean. He'll be here soon. Would you ladies like some coffee, as well?"

"Yes, please," I said.

Sam hurried into the living room where a fire crackled in the grate. Trouble darted off after her, and Bee and I busied ourselves slipping out of our coats and gloves as well.

"What do you think that was about?" Bee whispered.

"What?"

"She called the detective by his first name."

I shrugged. It wasn't any of my business. The only business we had now was celebrating Christmas, and, hopefully, helping the police find out who had done away with poor Jacobsen. Though I wasn't sure on that last part. Should we get involved? Or was it better to leave it to the professionals this time? How strange that this had happened. And how it had happened too—equally strange and alarming.

We hurried through to the living room and took up two armchairs in front of the fire. It was lovely and warm, and I lifted the poker and shifted the logs to release more of the heat. The embers sparked and swirled, and my thoughts wandered back to the lights on the Christmas tree in the center of town.

And the body underneath it.

Who might have wanted to do this? And why now? Why so close to Christmas? And in such a public fashion too. Surely, the killer had known this would make a scene and draw a lot of attention. Which meant they'd wanted that attention—after all, it would have been much easier just to hide the body, wouldn't it?

Easier in the sense that it would be harder for the detectives to find out who'd done it.

"Did you see Babcock?" Bee asked, quietly.

"Babcock?"

"Yeah, you know, the guy who was standing in for the mayor. Did you see his face after he'd switched on the lights and spotted the body?"

"I can't say I did, no."

"He was smiling," Bee whispered.

"Are you sure?"

"Absolutely," she replied and tied up her silver-gray hair. "Smiling from ear-to-ear like he'd just won the lottery, not seen a dead body."

"Well, if that's not suspicious then..."

"Exactly," Bee whispered, scooching forward a bit. "You know what we have to do, don't you?"

"Enjoy a cup of hot chocolate with mini-marsh-mallows?"

"Figure out who did it," she said, rolling her eyes at me. "This is perfect."

"Bee, excuse my ignorance here, but I'm failing to see how the death of the mayor is in any way 'perfect.' It's a tragedy."

"Oh, you know what I mean." Bee flapped her hands at me.

"I really don't."

"We're leaving Carmel Springs after Christmas, right? So, this is our opportunity to do one last good thing for the town and all the people in it. We can help them figure out who did this," Bee hissed. "We'll leave on a high note."

"Or we could just make Christmas cupcakes and hand them out?"

"You're not seriously planning on sitting on your laurels while there's a murderer around, are you?" Bee raised an eyebrow. "Because if that's the case, I don't know you at all."

In her past life—the one before she'd become my baker on the food truck—Bee had been a police officer. All these cases and dead bodies, well, they were like her Kryptonite. It was a miracle I hadn't figured out Bee's cop secret long before she told me just before Thanksgiving. She did have a penchant for munching on donuts and interfering. But then again, so did I.

"Rubes, come on. We should at least ask around. You know, sleuth out some clues."

"I'll think about it," I said. "For now, I just want to relax. It's almost Christmas." And indeed, the interior of the guesthouse had been decorated beautifully—tinsel hung from the corners of the halls and rooms and a tree had been decorated and positioned in front of the living room window, its lights flashing and casting merry glimmers across the floor. Mistletoe hung from the ceiling, as well, and one of the newer guests—Mr. Davidson—had already tried using it as an excuse to smooch me. Eugh.

Bee silenced herself and lifted the paper off the coffee table then settled into reading it. I was drawn in by the dance of the Christmas lights, the flicker and flash.

Why did the murderer leave the body under the tree?

All wrapped up. Like a Christmas present. Shudder-inducing.

The swinging doors to the kitchen opened, and Sam emerged carrying a tray stacked with three brimming cups. She handed them out, and we thanked her. The hot chocolate was delicious, and the mini-marshmallows had already started melting into sweet, white foam.

"Sorry it took me so long," Sam said, taking a seat in a third armchair closest to the fire and across from ours. "Shawn's already gone to bed, and I just got off a call with poor Ava."

"Ava, the mayor's wife?" I asked.

"Right. She's distraught. I could barely make out what she was saying over the phone. She's with the police, but she asked if she could come stay here for a few days. Apparently, she doesn't want to stay in her house. I think because of... you know, the memories. Poor Ian."

Ian was the mayor's first name. "She's coming to stay here?"

"That's what it looks like," Sam said. "Poor woman." A knock sounded at the front doors of the guesthouse, and Sam went to answer it, leaving us with that newest bombshell.

"Why would she be worried about where she stayed right after her husband was murdered?" Bee asked.

"I have no idea. It *is* strange. Maybe we should go talk to—"

Detective Martin entered the living room with Sam at his side and nodded to us both, effectively ending our suspicions and chatter. "Good evening, ladies. I'm here to ask a few questions and take some interviews. Sammy, would you mind waiting in the kitchen with Miss Holmes?"

"Of course. No problem," Sam said.

Sammy? Why's he calling her pet names? A flush of heat crept up my throat. Were the detective and Sam dating? And if they were, what did it matter? Surely, I wasn't jealous.

"Ruby?" Sam smiled at me.

She was pretty, after all. Mousy and a bit shy, but pretty in her own way. We were about the same age, her maybe a bit younger.

"Right, yeah. Coming." I took my hot chocolate with

me, choosing to focus instead on the case rather than my strange flushy-heat issue. I didn't have anything to be jealous about—I wasn't interested in the detective. I wasn't interested in anything or anyone other than baking and the food truck and maybe... solving another murder.

Four

"ARE YOU SURE THIS IS A GOOD IDEA?" I ASKED, AS we stepped out of the copy shop in Main Street, the stacks of invitations clasped to our chests. "I mean, the mayor did just…"

"Kick the bucket?" Bee suggested.

"Technically, he had his bucket kicked for him." I glanced left and right to ensure no one had eavesdropped. "But yeah, exactly. We don't want to upset anyone."

"Come on, Rubes, we've been planning this Christmas party for ages. I mean, we've hired out the town hall, for Pete's sake. We're not going to let this stop us, right?" Bee rifled through the invites. "It's going to be great. Think of it this way: our Christmas party will be a great send-off, and it will lift the morale in Carmel Springs."

"I guess," I replied.

But it had only been a day, a single day, since the mayor had been found underneath the Christmas tree in the center of town.

"This way. Let's hit the Corner Café. We can chat to Millie about taking out an ad for the party. She mentioned she'd be there this morning."

Bee was much more enthusiastic than she'd been at the start of our time together on the truck, and I couldn't bring myself to discourage her. She did have a point—hosting a party would help people cheer up and enjoy themselves this holiday season.

Though I wasn't positive that would help Ava Jacobsen. She'd arrived at the guesthouse early this morning. I'd spied her through the gap in my curtains at six. She'd been frail and blonde and red-eyed, and Sam had brought her into the guesthouse with much cooing and pats on the back.

Why doesn't she want to stay in her house? It's not like the murder happened there.

Or had it? Perhaps Ava Jacobsen knew something she wasn't—

"Ruby?"

"Right. Sorry! Coming." I skedaddled after Bee.

The Corner Café was one of the favorite hangout spots in Carmel Springs—especially in winter, when the beach was too chilly to visit and the pier was invaded by an icy ocean breeze. It sat on a corner—hence the name—along Main Street, right across from the town hall where we'd be hosting our party and near the green knoll that held the massive Christmas tree. Thankfully, it was now free of the corpse of the mayor.

Eugh, what a horrible thought.

The interior of the café was quaint with a wooden counter at the front, an assortment of tables and chairs, some of them mismatched, and pictures on the walls of the town from its inception. The aesthetic was fiercely small-town and welcoming. If a welcome could be fierce. Though, heavens, a lot of things had been fierce lately.

We handed out a few invites to the locals, receiving smiles and thanks in return, then spotted Millie sitting near the front windows and made our way over.

She had company. A woman who was... astounding in every sense of the word. She wore her hair a shimmering golden-red atop her head and a long fluffy red trench coat cinched at the waist to match it. Her makeup—gold eyeshadow and crimson lipstick—would've stood out on Broadway.

"Who's that?" I whispered.

"Let's find out." Bee walked over to the table and smiled at the women. "Good morning, Millie. And, oh, I don't think we've met, Mrs....?"

"It's Ms." The woman pursed those crimson lips and

speared first Bee and then me with a narrow-eyed stare. "Ms. Greta Gould. I'm surprised you haven't heard of me."

"Ms. Gould is one of the paper's primary investors," Millie said, though she didn't seem happy about it. Her eye kept twitching. Odd. "And good morning, ladies. What are you up to today?"

"We're handing out invitations to our party," I said, offering her one. "We'll be having it next week, just before Christmas."

"It's a farewell soiree, and everyone's invited." Bee gave Greta an invitation, as well.

The fabulous Ms. Gould studied the invite like it had insulted her merely by existing. She pursed and rolled her lips. "I see." She put the slip of paper down, gingerly. "Well, that's nice for you, but Millie and I were just—"

"It's fine, Greta," Millie said. "I can talk about it later. Join us, please, Ruby. Bee." Her tone was tinged with desperation. Goodness, what was that about? Did Millie not want to spend time with the mysterious Greta?

Color me intrigued. And hungry. "Don't mind if we do," I said. "I'm starved. I'd kill for a scone right about now."

A few of the nearby diners dropped their forks or gasped. *Poor choice of words.*

"Sorry," I called out, waving a hand. "I didn't mean it like that. I'm just, um, hungry."

Bee and I dragged two chairs to the table and sat down next to each other—elbow space was at a minimum, both because we were squished into the short side of the table, and because Ms. Gould didn't seem willing to move her glittering handbag out of our way.

"Hmm, let's see what's good." Bee swept up a menu and started perusing, but her gaze lifted over the edge of the card and wandered between Millie and Greta.

"Are you sure this is all right?" I asked, trying not to nudge Greta's handbag. "If you two are busy with important work…"

"Now that you mention it," Greta started.

"No, no. There's nothing too important to discuss. Greta was just checking in on the paper's circulation dates. She wants us to publish two times a week instead of one." Millie had blanched. "But, of course, we're not sure we can meet those types of deadlines or come up with enough content in such a short amount of—"

"Now that's just a load of steaming hot trash, Millie, and you know it." Greta had lifted a finger tipped in a crimson nail. She jabbed it in Millie's direction. "There's plenty of content. It's just you don't want to publish it."

"Greta, we have guests."

"You're avoiding my eyes, Millie. You won't look at

me. Why is that?" Greta's voice reminded me of a foghorn in the night. Again, folks at their tables turned and peered over at us.

"That's ridiculous. I'm not avoiding anything. We won't be able to publish twice a week without the necessary staff and writers and, frankly, our printing presses are just... Look, everything's going digital nowadays, and running both an e-zine and a newspaper is too much work for the amount of staff we have. Surely you can understand that, Greta?"

"No, I can't. You just need to work harder. There's plenty of news to spread around. Cripes, there have been about twenty murders in the last few months."

"Five," I said, helpfully. "Just five."

"And people want updates on what's going on," Greta said. "You can fill them in on all the juicy gossip with a biweekly paper. If you thin it out a bit, so what? You'll become the go-to crime information source. We'll be influencers."

"Influencers?" Millie frowned. "I'm not sure what that means."

"Of course you're not." Greta swept a few strands of hair back from her eyes. "You're short-sighted, and that's exactly why I'll be leading the charge at the paper."

"Greta, that's not possible. You're an investor, not the owner of the—"

"I bought it," Greta said, triumphantly. "The paper. I bought the paper. We'll be rebranding it and publishing as I see fit, and if you don't like that, Millie, well, I'll find someone who does like it." She paused and laughed. "Everyone is so short-sighted in this town. It's people like you and that mayor who get killed because of it. I suggest you re-evaluate how you do business." Greta snatched up her bag and rose from the table. She left the Corner Café, trailing a cloud of pungent perfume.

"Good heavens," I said. "Millie, are you all right?"

Millie trembled in her seat, either from self-contained rage or upset. "I'll be fine. She won't get away with this. She can't." Our friend got up and collected her bag. "I'm sorry, ladies, but I'm not in the mood to eat anymore. I'll... talk to you later."

"Of course, Millie," I said. "I hope you feel better. Everything's going to be fine." Would it be, though? It seemed like this Greta woman was on the warpath, and it didn't matter who stood in her way.

Five

After the strange "Gould Incident" at the Corner Café, I'd lost my appetite as well. My brain had taken up the charge: figure out how to help Millie. But then, there were so many charges to take up lately, what with the party coming up, the death of the mayor, and now Millie's impending loss of the paper. It was difficult to pick one.

I led the way up the front steps of the Oceanside Guesthouse. The doors were shut tight against the miserable weather—overcast, the odd splotch of rain on the rooftop or pathway—and I took a minute to collect myself before entering.

What was this Greta woman up to? Why had she decided to change the publication schedule of the paper? And what was the obsession with the murders and crime?

Did she want to solve the murder? But no, she didn't exactly strike me as the type who'd look out for Carmel Springs' best interests.

And you are?

It was silly. I'd sworn I would never rest my head in any guesthouse for too long, but this place had grown to be home.

"Are you OK, Ruby?" Bee touched a hand to my shoulder.

"Yes, why?"

"You've been staring at the front door for two minutes. I figured you had something important on your mind."

I paused, grasping the last of our invitations tighter in my gloved fingertips. "I don't know, Bee. I guess I'm just... I don't know."

"That's about as clear as a cake batter."

"Sorry." I managed a laugh. "I'm confused about a lot of things. We're leaving soon, and we've got the party coming up, and I'm sad but excited about going. A new adventure is always good, right? But leaving Carmel Springs..."

Bee looped her arm through mine and led me to the swinging seat on the porch. "This is why we're going to solve the mayor's murder," she said, quietly. "It will be our last farewell to the town."

"I'm not so sure that's a good idea, Bee. What if we mess it up?" Tainting the image of the last few months we'd had in Carmel Springs would be a terrible leaving present.

"What are you afraid of?" Bee asked. "You're usually excited about investigating mysteries."

"I'm not sure." Maybe she was right. I didn't want to figure it out for fear that I would get drawn into staying here another month. That was what had happened after we'd solved Owen Pelletier's murder. And as much as I loved this town and all its people, it was time to move on.

I had an itch in the soles of my feet, a building worry that if I stayed too long here, I'd grow roots. And then the folks in town would get to know me and find out about my past, and the stares and whispers would start.

She can't keep a man. Her fiancé ran away. Her fiancé couldn't stand to be around her for a second longer.

"Look," Bee said, "I don't know what's going through that head of yours, but I can assure you that this will be the best Christmas ever, and that solving this case will only make it better. Let's help these people." She tapped her chin and pointed at me. "Without Detective Martin finding out."

"Right." We got off the swinging chair, and I caught Bee's arm. "Promise me something, though?"

"Anything."

"Promise me that we will definitely leave town after Christmas. Even if I don't want to."

"Is that what's bothering you?" Bee shook her head. "Rubes, after this town, we'll be adventuring in another one. That's been the plan all along. Don't let that worry your little old head. I promise."

"Thanks."

After that, it was easier to go inside and strip off my outerwear. Sam had seated herself behind the reception desk and was working on her accounts—Trouble the growing kitty had decided lying across the pages and scratching at her pen nib was the best way to increase her productivity.

"Tea and cookies in the living room," Sam said, smiling at us and darting her pen away from Trouble's calico paw. "But, um, just be mindful... Ava's in there. She's not feeling that great."

Bee and I exchanged the briefest of glances. The spouse was always the main suspect in murder cases, and this was our chance to get inside information.

"We'll try to be—" I started.

A man exited into the hall, and I cut off. He wore his hair long and held back in a ponytail. A single golden hoop earring hung from his right ear. A modern-day pirate without the peg leg.

"How's she doing, Jerry?" Sam asked the guy.

"She's as to be expected. Not doing great, but what can we do? She just needs to rest and relax."

"Hi," I said, holding out a hand. "I'm Ruby."

"How rude of me," Sam said. "Sorry, this is Jerry Flagg. He was the mayor's assistant. Jerry, this is Bee, and this is Ruby. They're guests at the Oceanside and very good friends of mine."

Bee shook Jerry's hand next. "You're here for Ava?" she asked.

"Just trying to comfort her. The mayor and I got kinda close working together, and Ava's a friend. I can't imagine what she's going through." He checked his watch. "I'd better get going. The town committee is holding a closed-doors meeting regarding the mayoral position."

"Nice to meet you," I called after him.

"Interesting dude," Bee said, gesturing near her ear. "I didn't know hoop earrings were still in fashion."

"Were they ever in fashion?" I asked.

Bee chuckled, and we waved to Sam and headed into the living room, seeking out our cookies and tea. Gosh, Shawn, the new chef at the Oceanside, was so great at baking and cooking, the smells drifting through the guest-house had me hungry all day and night.

Mrs. Jacobsen sat in one of the armchairs by the fire, lifting a teacup to her lips. She shook badly and spilled golden liquid to her lap then muttered and put down the cup on the coffee table. "Silly," she whispered to herself, shaking her blonde head. "Terrible. I'm so..."

"Sorry," Bee said. "Mind if we join you? We're frozen to the bone."

Ava jumped as if she'd been poked. "Oh! Oh, hello. I didn't see you there."

"Evidently," Bee replied.

I stepped on the toe of her boot. Bee wasn't the best at interacting emotionally with people. Sarcasm was her go-to response.

"How are you feeling, Ava?" I asked, taking the armchair to her left. Bee took the one to her right and put out her hands to the fire.

"Cold and unhappy." Ava sniffed and lifted a crumpled Kleenex. She dabbed underneath her eyes, and bits of the white tissue dropped off. "It's just so... it's beyond belief. I don't understand why anyone would have wanted to hurt Ian. He was a good man. A nice man. He did his best for this town, and the fact that someone would even conceive of doing this is just..." She sniffled, and a single tear tracked down her cheek.

"We're so sorry for your loss," I said.

"Thank you," Ava replied. "I'm glad to be here. Everyone in this guesthouse has been friendly and welcoming. I just couldn't stay in that house a second longer."

"Why?" Bee asked.

Ava blinked at the abrupt question. "Because that was where we shared our happiest memories. And staying there and reliving them is too painful for me." She wiped the tear away. "I don't know how I'm going to live without Ian. He was such a rock."

So far, all we'd learned was that Mayor Jacobsen had been liked by all. And that he might have had an enemy in the form of the Babcock. Millie had mentioned that the other day—that the Babcock had lost to the mayor in the elections.

I chewed on my lip. "Ava, have you spoken to the police about what's happened?"

"Yes, of course. That Detective Martin came by and interviewed me." The briefest flash of anger crossed Ava's expression—a pulling down at the corners of the lips, wrinkles arching between her brows. But the sorrow returned a second later. "He was rough and too much. I didn't like talking to him. He asked the stupidest questions."

"What type of questions?" Bee asked.

"That's really none of your business," Ava said, coldly.

This was the reaction Bee incited in people. "Sorry, Ava," I said, "we didn't mean to upset you. It's just that—" I struggled for a reason and latched onto one. "The cops in Carmel Springs try their best, but they haven't exactly had a great track record over the past while."

"Oh, I heard. I believe that Jones, may he rest in peace, locked you up for a night a few weeks ago."

"That's right," I said. "We've made a habit of looking into these cases ourselves, you know?"

"Oh." Ava turned her gaze to the fire.

"Ava, can you think of anyone who might have wanted to harm your husband?" Bee asked, measuring her tone this time. "Anyone at all?"

The mayor's wife remained silent for a few minutes, the popping of the logs in the fireplace seemed louder than usual. "Maybe," she whispered. "I don't want to falsely accuse anyone, but I'll tell you that the only person my husband didn't like was that butcher. Babcock."

"The Babcock," I breathed.

"That's right," Ava said. "He threatened my Ian on several occasions."

"With violence?"

"No, nothing like that," Ava whispered, quickly, her eyes dancing now, more alive than they'd been a few minutes ago, as if the gossip had invigorated her. "He threatened to steal the position of mayor from Ian. If anyone had it out for him, it was the butcher."

And there we had it, our first real lead.

A butcher's threat. Could the mystery be that simple to solve?

Six

"Are you sure this is OK?" Sam asked, wringing her hands as she stood in front of the reception desk in the Oceanside. "I don't want to impose. I'm sure you ladies have much more important things to do today."

"It's no imposition." I patted her on the shoulder. "We planned on taking a walk today, anyway. Maybe stopping by the Lobster Shack to see if they've got anything interesting on special? Right Bee?"

"Of course," Bee said. "As if you could ever impose. You're our friend."

"Yes, and you're doing a really good thing for Ava." Even though Ava was one of our prime suspects since she was the spouse of the deceased. But running an errand for Sam was a good thing to do for our friend, and it helped that that errand would take us to another suspect.

"It's an inconvenience, though," Sam continued, lifting Trouble into her arms and stroking his furry head. He purred and pressed himself into her hand. "I wish Mr. Babcock would just allow us to book our turkeys online."

"Or, how about everyone just fetches their turkeys on the twenty-third?" Bee asked.

Sam gave a scandalized gasp, and Trouble batted her chin. "And risk not getting a turkey at all? No, Bee, the booking system at our local butcher's is the *only* way you can ensure a happy Christmas lunch or dinner in Carmel Springs." She licked her lips. "The Babcock might have his flaws, but this system isn't one of them. Are you sure you want to go?"

"We're sure."

"Forget about it," Bee said and winked.

We headed out of the guesthouse, our coats fluffy and warm and our gloves thick, and made our way toward the food truck. There wasn't a chance I'd walked all the way to the butcher's in this weather. I was big on sightseeing, but a couple minutes out in the cold had already turned me into Rudolph the Red-nosed Reindeer.

The food truck's heating warmed the interior of the cab and misted up the window, so I rolled one of mine down and let a sliver of cool air in.

Five minutes later, we parked outside the butcher's shop. The windows had been sprayed with stenciled

Christmas décor—snowflakes, reindeer outlines, and Santa's sleigh—while specials were proclaimed in the window.

"Book your turkey before it's too late." Bee read the words off a clapboard that had been placed out in the street. "The best turkey you'll ever eat. Now if that's not marketing genius, I don't know what is."

"It's a small town, Bee. I don't think he has much competition."

"Blatantly obvious. Look how many people are in there."

My best baker and friend was right. The inside of the butcher's shop was packed full of people, and there didn't seem to be a line of any sort heading from the main counter at the front.

"We'd better get in there," I said. "We don't want to miss our shot. Sam will have a panic attack if she doesn't get her turkey."

"She'll probably be more panicked than Ava is about her husband," Bee whispered.

I didn't comment. Apparently, Bee thought Ava's grief wasn't sorrowful enough. Or she was just being her usual suspicious self. Regardless, we pulled the door open and slipped into the crowd.

It was hot inside, and the scent of salts, meat, and spices clogged the air between the milling people of

Carmel Springs. A few of them mumbled or chatted, waiting their turn, perhaps grumbling about the wait, but the others? Why, they were focused on the spectacle that was the Babcock himself.

Clayton was up on the front counter, the thick soles of his rubbery boots squeaking as he walked back and forth, talking at speed. "—have all been scared, and I'll be honest, I'm scared too," he was saying. "But I'm glad that so many of you are here today. It shows that nothing, not even the horrifying death of the man who was supposed to care for this town, can keep us apart." He paused for effect.

"That's hardly sanitary," Bee whispered. "His boots on that counter. Should we really book a turkey from here?"

"I don't see that we have another choice. The General Store doesn't stock fowl."

"The only thing that's foul around here is his boots on that counter." Bee grimaced. "As a woman in the food industry, I find this disturbing."

"Not nearly as disturbing as you should find the death of the mayor," I whispered.

It was a good way to bring our thoughts back to our second reason for coming to Babcock's butchery—he was a suspect. The sworn enemy of the deceased mayor. Sworn enemies were a big deal in Carmel Springs—the town had a rich history of them and their antics.

The door to the butchery opened, and a glamorous

woman, ensconced in a cloud of perfume, entered. It was Greta Gould, the wannabe Broadway star from the Corner Café. She hovered near the entrance, her eyes narrowed as she studied the Babcock.

"—look after this town. Let's face it, folks, not everyone's cut out to deliver the quality service that I am. You all know from your experiences in this butchery that I am the pro at giving people exactly what they want when they want it."

Nobody nodded. In fact, a couple people looked mildly annoyed. Nobody had gotten what they'd wanted this morning, it seemed.

"How does one book a turkey?" I whispered.

"I guess we have to talk to Mr. Braggy Pants," Bee replied. "If he ever stops talking."

"The thing is," the Babcock continued, "you all deserve someone who'll look after your best interests. There's no one in this town who could possibly say that Mayor Jacobsen did anything to uplift us. And if they did say that, they'd be lying. Carmel Springs has just entered a trying time. We're in huge need of guidance, and we all know that I am the one who can provide that guidance."

A shifting nearby drew my attention from the braggart Babcock. Greta had a magnificent, golden-gloved hand pressed to the glass front door. Her eyes, done in dramatic smoky eyeshadow, were narrowed at the Babcock, and the more he spoke about his aspirations to be mayor and how bad Mayor Jacobsen had been for the town, the thinner her lips grew.

I nudged Bee as surreptitiously as I could and nodded to Greta.

"—think that I'm the only candidate who could possibly take Jacobsen's place. I know that I'm going to bring to you exactly what you need as the good citizens off Carmel Springs."

Greta's mouth was now a bitter slash. She pushed the door open and slipped out into the street, introducing a cold gust of wind into the shop.

I shivered.

The door slapped shut, but the noise didn't deter the ongoing speech. "—no more crime! No more murders. With me at the helm, you'll finally be safe from the vicious evildoers who stalk our town."

A few people had perked up at the mention of murder, but mostly, people were still annoyed, pulling off their gloves or fiddling with their collars in the growing heat inside the shop. And what about Greta's behavior? Was she just as frustrated as we were? Had she left because she'd wanted to book a turkey?

Greta doesn't seem the type who'd be into cooking turkeys. But wait, was there a type for that? Anyone could cook. Not everyone could cook well.

"Now, I know most of you are here to book your turkeys," the Babcock said, and people shuffled and finally started acting eager. "But if you'll give me just another twenty minutes of your time, I can explain my fifty-point plan for the—"

"What do we do?" I whispered.

"Wait, I guess," Bee replied, "I hate to say it, but we've got to listen to Babcock if we want to save Christmas at the Oceanside."

My gaze traveled to the door, but it remained empty of glamor or Greta. Why had she been in here? And why had she left in such a rush?

Seven

It took another hour before we finally got to the front of the line in the butcher's shop and booked our turkey. By the time we'd squeezed out of the shop, a full queue had started outside the door, and the folks still waiting to make their bookings inside seemed on the brink of rioting.

Suffice to say, everyone had grown sick of the Babcock's grandiose plans and self-aggrandizement. But no one had the chops to put him in his place, apart from maybe Bee. I'd had to step on her toe and pinch her elbow to get her to keep quiet. The last thing we needed was to make a murder suspect an enemy. Buttering them up was key.

Then again, Babcock had buttered himself up with the

talk so fully, I doubted there was a stick of butter left in the state.

"All right," Bee said, once we'd gotten back into the food truck and switched on the heating. "That was both nightmarish and interesting."

"It's fair to say that Babcock has a vested interest in being the mayor."

"But does he want that enough to murder for the office?" Bee asked.

"That's what we have to find out." I started up the engine and waited for it to warm up. The windshield misted from the heat, and, once again, I cracked a window.

"Why don't we head to the Lobster Shack?" Bee asked. "I'm starved, and I heard they're doing a hot lobster chowder. Millie raved about it the other night, and I've had a hankering ever since."

"Sounds great!"

Fifteen minutes later, we had a spot next to the windows that looked out on the gorgeous cove and the choppy waters. The inside of the Lobster Shack was decorated with buoys and had a rustic feel, but the food was absolutely exquisite.

I lifted my menu off the table and perused. Chowder was great, but I was always looking for something new to try.

"Ooh, this lobster melt looks delicious," I said, tapping the menu card. "What do you think?"

"We should get fried clams for starters." Bee licked her lips. "I'm so hungry I can barely think straight."

Right on cue, the waiter appeared to serve us. She took our orders with a smile and returned shortly after with a breadbasket, a soda for me, and a chocolate milkshake for Bee.

I sipped my soda, turning toward the window and propping my chin in my hand. Maine was so gorgeous, I'd miss it once we were gone. Only a few more weeks, and we'd be on our way out onto another small town, shoot, maybe even another state.

"Getting sad?" Bee asked, between slurps of her milkshake.

"A little. Maybe."

"Don't be. We're going on another adventure. And we have each other."

I met Bee's gaze and grinned. It was good to have a friend like her. Honestly, she was the first person I'd relied on in a long time. Since Daniel had broken my trust entirely and proven to me that most of the time, people couldn't be trusted.

Some of them. I trusted Sam. And Shawn. And perhaps even Detective Martin—though that was debatable. I trusted him as a person, but did I trust him as a detective? Of course. To a certain extent. But I itched to figure out what had happened to Mayor Jacobsen.

That was likely because I had the ever-present urge to find out the truth. Peel back the layers of—

"Are you all right?" Bee asked. "You haven't touched the garlic bread."

I chuckled. "I'm fine. I was just thinking about the mayor." I lifted a slice of bread out of the basket. It was stringy with cheese and dripping golden butter.

"Hmm, I've been pondering it too."

"What are your thoughts?" I asked, scooching closer to the edge of my chair.

Bee did a scooch of her own, and we put out heads together. "We don't have any real suspects except for Clayton Babcock and Ava. We disregarded the wife the last time around, and that was a mistake. We should keep our eyes on her."

"But what would her motive have been?" I asked. "She's clearly upset over her husband's passing, and there hasn't even been a whisper about marital problems."

"Hasn't there? I think we'll have to talk to Millie before we decide on that."

"Poor Millie," I said. "She's got enough on her plate at the moment. You heard Greta the other day. She was adamant she'd change the whole paper around. Being the editor is Millie's life."

Bee gave a doleful nod. "True. Millie deserves better than that. But we're getting off-track. What about the Babcock?"

"I find it really weird that everyone calls him that. It really makes him sound like a mythical creature."

"Well, he certainly gives speeches like he's some type of ancient all-knowing wizard," Bee said.

"He clearly had a motive. He's going to try get the mayoral position," I whispered. "And what will that mean?"

"That the folks of Carmel Springs will be condemned to listening to his dulcet tones at every event for the foreseeable future. A fate worse than death." Bee finished off her milkshake and pressed it to one side of the table. "The man loves the sound of his own voice. Could that be a sign?"

"What do you mean?"

"You know, narcissists love the sound of their own voice too. Maybe he has Narcissistic Personality Disorder. A lot of murderers have it."

"That's an assumption we can't afford to make," I said, my belly growling for lunch. I opened my handbag to distract myself and brought out my notepad. I pressed it flat to the tabletop and wrote the mayor's name at the top, then underlined it. I drew a line down the page then wrote "the Babcock" and circled that.

"The enemy," Bee said, leaning over. "But what about Ava?"

I drew another connection to the mayor's name and wrote Ava's with two question marks next to it and the word "motive" in brackets. She didn't have one yet. Unless there had been a will that her husband had written her into.

The waiter appeared next to our table with our fried clam starter, and I squirreled the notepad out of sight. We thanked her and started stuffing our faces with the clams, losing our train of thought and conversation.

The food was too good to worry too much about the murder now. It was Christmas. We had a party coming up and the last few days to enjoy with our friends. Should we really spend it on the murder? Bee was determined. And I was tired of doubting myself.

"These are so good," I said.

Bee's chowder and my lobster melt came next, and we gorged ourselves on the food, the tender lobster meat sending a shockwave of dopamine through me. So divine. After, we paid our bill, dabbed our lips with napkins, and headed out onto the pier.

I fiddled with the fingers of my gloves, seating them properly on my hands in the chill outside.

"Look there," Bee whispered, grasping my forearm.

Over at the far end of the pier, standing next to one of

the benches, was Detective Martin. He had a notepad out and tapped a pen against it, while talking to Greta Gould.

"What's she doing with him?" I asked.

"She has to be a suspect. Why else would she be questioned? I didn't see her at the tree-lighting ceremony, did you?"

"Not that I can remember," I said.

"And you'd remember someone like Greta." Bee gestured vaguely toward her hair. "I mean she's hardly the wilting wallflower type."

Greta shook her head, adamant about *something,* as she spoke to Detective Martin. But adamant about what? And why wouldn't Martin just have asked her back to the station? Surely, that would've been more comfortable for both of them. Unless she had refused?

"Why do you think she's a suspect?" I asked. "Could it have something to do with the Babcock? You saw her in the butchery today."

"Yeah." Bee pursed her lips. "Though we can't possibly find out why without—"

Detective Martin looked up from his notepad and caught my eye. Quickly, Bee and I averted our gazes. I feigned an interest in the pier's wooden railing and pretended to comment on it. Bee followed my lead and bent over to examine it.

"Ladies," Detective Martin said, stopping beside us.

"Oh, hello, detective," I said. "I didn't see you there."

He harrumphed. Was he becoming more like the recently departed Detective Jones, or was that just me? He'd gone crotchety ever since he'd started taking over these cases. "You didn't see me there. Where didn't you see me?"

I glanced past him, but the bench where Greta had been seated was empty now. I gave an awkward laugh but didn't answer.

"How's your investigation going, detective?" Bee asked, brusquely. "Any new leads?"

"You'll find out when the rest of the public does," Martin said. "I suggest you two ladies get out of the cold. Weather's not for tourists. You're liable to freeze your fingers off."

"Thanks for the advice."

"It was a strong suggestion." Martin paused. "The other being that you stay well away from this murder case."

"We weren't doing anything," I protested.

But the detective had already started off down the pier, settling his police beanie onto his head and tugging it down around his ears.

"Well, looks like we're on our own on this one," I said.

Bee slipped her arm into mine. "Wouldn't have it any

other way. Now let's get back to the Oceanside before I freeze my fingers off, as Martin so aptly put it."

Eight

THE FOLLOWING DAY, BEE AND I HEADED OUT TO the town hall, our spirits only slightly dampened by the icy weather. We were set on making this the best possible send-off in the spirit of Christmas, both for ourselves and for our friends.

It was difficult, though, to put aside the questions and thoughts revolving around the mayor's murder. The entire town was abuzz with the news, and speculation was rife. Posters had been put against the wrought iron lampposts—headline news decrying the ongoing investigation.

Even the weather hadn't stopped folks from coming out to talk about the murder. The Corner Café was the hotspot of all the activity, and given that it was right across from the town hall and the Christmas tree on the grassy—

now snowy—knoll, it was the perfect place to stop for coffee.

Bee and I dipped inside and stripped off our gloves. We joined the line that led toward the coffee machine.

"Are you ready to get decorating?" I asked.

"I was born ready," Bee replied. "I need something to keep me busy. I miss baking, and when I'm not, all I think about is the case."

"Me too."

The line shifted, and we gave our orders to the barista and paid then stepped aside to wait. "You know," I said, "I'm thinking we could use some help with the decorating. Maybe, we should get hold of the decorating committee from the Carmel Springs council?"

"Way ahead of you, Rubes." Bee pointed toward the town hall.

Outside it, a small group of people stood waiting. One of them was a familiar, a young man with a ponytail and a thick fluffy coat.

"Who is that?" I asked. "He looks so familiar."

"That's Jerry. He's the head of the decorating committee, and he was the mayor's assistant," she said. "Naturally, he can't assist anyone now."

"Oh, he was the one who was being nice to Ava at the guesthouse."

"Right," Bee said. "Well, he's been helpful, so far." She

checked her watch. "We're meeting him in about five minutes."

"Does he have the keys to the town hall?" It was shameful on my part, but I hadn't had much involvement in organizing the decoration of the town hall or even the booking of the venue. I'd spent the last few days cleaning out the truck and occasionally getting emotional over leaving Carmel Springs.

"Yes, he does," Bee said and patted me on the back. "Don't worry, Rubes. I've got everything under control."

"You're a star."

Bee flashed me her signature gap-toothed grin. We collected our coffees from a tired barista who still offered us a "Merry Christmas" and a smile.

We headed out across the street. Snow fell. A thin layer had gathered on the ground this morning, and it seemed it would only get thicker today. I *had* been dreaming of a Neil Diamond "White Christmas." The cold was manageable when it was this beautiful. A thin dusting of snow had already attached itself to the branches of the communal Christmas tree.

"Hello," Bee called, as we crossed the road.

Jerry Flagg smiled at her and shook her hand. "Bee. It's good to see you again. And you're..."

"Ruby," I said and took his hand next. "Thanks for helping us, Mr. Flagg."

"Please, call me Jerry," he said and wiped his hand off on his jacket after our handshake. "And it's a great pleasure. We're happy to help. It's a fantastic idea to have a Christmas party, and from what I've heard, everyone wants to come." Jerry stamped his feet in his boots. "And I've got even better news. I chatted with the town council and did a bit of convincing, and they've agreed to help with the costs of the party!"

"That's amazing," I said, my heart filling with joy. It wasn't that I'd been worried about paying for the party, especially as a farewell event, but the extra funding would help us make this an even bigger deal. "Thank you so much."

"That's totally my pleasure," Jerry said. "I'm always happy to help out around town."

"Wow." Bee and I exchanged grins.

"All right, so are you ladies ready to get started?" Jerry asked, clapping his gloved hands together. The other committee members gathered behind him, eager to get started—or just to get out of the cold. "Let's go!" Jerry dipped his hand into his pocket and removed the key to the town hall doors. He loped over to them, opened up, then stepped inside and hit the lights.

I inhaled sharply.

I'd half-expected we'd find another body in the hall. But no, it was empty except for the usual chairs lined up facing the podium where the mayor would sometimes speak.

"All right," Jerry said, "I hope you ladies don't mind if I take charge?"

"Not at all," I replied.

"Within reason." Bee removed her gloves. "We've got some decoration plans, but we've still got to visit the General Store to stock up on tinsel."

"Right, of course." Jerry had brought out his phone and tapped on the screen. "We'll see what we can do about that." His fingers flew over the phone's touch keyboard as he typed notes. "All right, everyone, let's get these chairs packed up and placed in the stage wings. Got it?"

The door to the hall creaked, and Detective Martin entered wearing a thick leather jacket over his uniform. He swept his beanie off his head and came over. "What's going on here, Flagg?"

"Jerry's helping us set up for the party," I said. "It's going to be—"

"I'm afraid that's not happening," the detective replied, stiffly. "There won't be any Christmas parties. We're shutting the town down."

"You're what?" Bee's eyes widened.

I held back a gasp.

"Shutting the town down in what sense?" Jerry asked.

"I've just come from talking with the council

members. They held a private vote a half an hour ago upon my urging. There will be no festivities or parties, no celebrations in the open, and no mass gatherings until the murder of Mayor Jacobsen has been resolved."

"That's not possible," I said. "Jerry's just gotten the council to help us fund our party. Why would they—?"

"That's not my problem," Martin said. "I have to do what's best for the residents of this town, and if that means shutting down every caroling club and Christmas party, so be it."

Nine

"I can't believe this is happening," I said, as we piled out of the town hall.

Detective Martin stood next to Jerry, breathing down his neck as he ensured the town hall was locked up, and the committee members were in the process of dispersing.

"Neither can I," Bee hissed. "There's no way we're going to let this happen."

"What do you suggest?" I asked, walking a couple steps away from the detective so he wouldn't overhear. *I can't believe I thought he was cute. Oof, now, that was out of left field.* "We can't go against direct orders."

"Yes," Bee said, "but we can solve the case. There's no way they can stop us from celebrating with our friends if we remove the threat."

"Of course." The threat. "They wouldn't shut the

town down unless they were scared the murderer would strike again. But why? Who would be the target?"

"I don't know." Bee brushed snowflakes from her hair. "But I'm sure we can figure this out."

Could we? It felt, sometimes, like all the past solved cases had been lucky breaks. Or that we'd taken a step too far and been fortunate enough not to either get arrested or hurt ourselves. *Sheesh, since when are you full of self-doubt?*

"We just have to nail down our suspect list," Bee said. "And maybe check out the crime scene once things have, you know, calmed down."

Another sprinkle of doubt frosted my mind-donut. "Do you really think it's best to get involved? I mean, the police—"

"Are y'all talking about the murder?" A woman spoke directly in my ear, and I jumped about a foot in the air.

I landed with a hiccup of a yelp and spun toward her.

She was short and thin as a rake, with long fingers that twitched at her sides. Her hair was tucked up underneath a polka-dotted beanie, and her smile was yellow-toothed and broad. "Hi," she said. "I'm Misty Lamone."

"Misty Lamone," I repeated, unable to tear my focus from her. It was the way she carried herself, and the strange outfit she'd put together—a lime green coat, the beanie, and then a pair of purple-striped pants.

"Well, Misty Lamone," Bee said, "you've just interrupted our conversation rather rudely. Is there something you want?" I could always trust Bee to say it exactly as it was.

Misty glanced back at the town hall, and I did too. Most of the folks there had dispersed, but Martin appeared to be in deep conversation—or argument—with Jerry.

"Let's step around the corner," Misty whispered. "I think I can help you solve the case."

"You heard that?" I asked.

"Uh, yeah? You weren't exactly whispering." Misty rolled her eyes—she had on purple eyeliner. "Look, I know who you two are. You're the leaf peepers who do that food truck baking stuff, right?"

"Right. But what's that—" I started.

"And you solved a few murders around town," Misty said. "Let's just say, if I saw something, and I didn't want to talk to the police about it, but I did want the murder to be, you know, solved... who would I talk to?"

"A couple of leaf peepers, apparently." Bee peered past Misty at the detective again. "All right, let's step around the corner and check out the Christmas tree."

A mixture of excitement and nerves erupted in my belly as we walked around the corner with Misty, across the street and toward the snowy knoll and the massive Christmas tree.

The tree was absolutely stunning. I hadn't had the chance to admire it the other night, given the circumstances, but up close, the special touches, including the tiny glittery red buoys in honor of the lobster industry that kept the town alive, brought warmth and comfort, as did the flashing lights and silver white star on top.

Misty stopped in front of it, rubbing her arms. "All right, that's better. Now he can't hear us."

"Why don't you want to talk to the police?" Bee was an ex-cop. No doubt, Misty seemed pretty darn suspicious to her. She did to me too.

"Let's just say, I have a spotty history with them."

"Define spotty," Bee replied. "You, uh, ran into trouble with the law? You did something wrong?"

"Look, if you're worried that I'm somehow involved, you can breathe easy. I wasn't. But I was around when the tree was being erected before the murder, and I think I saw something."

"Before the murder?" I asked.

Bee put up a purple gloved hand. "Wait a minute. First, tell us exactly what you did wrong that you're not interested in talking to the police."

Misty sniffed, her cheeks red either in defiance or from the cold. "Look," she said, "either you want this information or you don't. I ain't gonna hang around and talk to you if you're going to try to pry into my private business." She jerked her head to one side. "Now, do you want the information or not?"

Bee pursed her lips.

"We want the information," I said, quickly.

"Good. OK, so the stage was right here, in front of the knoll. And the tree is here obviously. We spent the whole day decorating. They made me do the back," Misty said, rolling her eyes again—apparently, that was her signature move. "Come on. Around here." She had a strange gait, a sort of "hunchback of Notre Dame" walk without the hunchback.

"See." Misty gestured to the tree. "I was on this side hanging up the baubles. Anyway, I took a break because trimming a tree is hard work. I was sitting right here." She scuffed the ground with her shoe. "With a view of the church over there." She pointed to the building directly across from the grassy patch.

The back of the church was hidden behind snow-dusted fir trees and a low slung stone wall that was topped in wrought iron spikes. The gate itself was wrought iron too and locked with a thick padlock.

"Anyway, so I'm sitting here, having a smoke, and I saw this... person. At the time, I thought they were watching me, but I wasn't sure."

"A person? What did they look like?" I asked, my heart

skipping a beat. Could it have been the killer, casing out the murder scene prior to doing the deed? *Eugh. I hate how that sounds.*

"That's the thing. I didn't see their face. They were sort of crouched down, peeking over the edge of the stone part of the wall. They had a beanie on, and all I saw were their eyes."

"Did you see what color they were?"

"No, sorry. They were wearing sunglasses. But they did have on black gloves. It was so weird that I sort of just stubbed out my cigarette and ran over to the Corner Café to grab a drink of coffee. By the time I got back, they were gone." Misty shrugged. "I don't know if it's worth much, but I thought someone ought to know."

"You really should tell the police," I said.

"No. No way. And if you tell them, I'll say I have no idea what you're talking about, all right? So, just butt out of my life." Misty gave them both a final venomous stare then marched around the tree, her boots crunching in the snow.

"Wow," I said.

"Wow indeed. It looks like we finally have another lead."

My gaze shifted to the back of the church again. Bee was right. We had a starting point and information that

Detective Martin didn't. That meant it was even less likely he'd catch us if we did investigate the churchyard.

"What do you say, Rubes? Are we doing this?"

I took a final breath. *Surely you can't do this. You'll get caught. Or you won't be able to solve the case or...* "We're doing it," I said, setting my jaw.

Ten

The lights from the Christmas tree sparkled next to the town hall. The decorations were perfect, from the baubles and mistletoe trimmings to the sparkling star on the very top of the tree, but the warm Christmassy vibe didn't change the fact that Bee and I were frozen and dressed in black.

We tried to affect a natural attitude as we approached the back of the church. The lights in the street were still on, but the lampposts were far apart, and the last of the late-night shoppers in the center of town had already rushed back to their homes, their arms laden with parcels.

The night sky was shrouded in a blanket of clouds and all was deathly quiet because of the snow. *Ooh, maybe don't think of it as "deathly."* After all, we were fast approaching the same stone wall where Misty had claimed she'd seen a strange person casing out the Christmas tree.

Could one case out a Christmas tree? The thought was ridiculous.

"I'm frozen," I whispered.

"Me too. But this will be worth it in the end," Bee said, eyeing the church's gate. It was spiked, but it wasn't too tall. "If we can get over."

"We'll get over. You're only as old as you feel."

"For a second, I thought you said 'cold' as I feel. Because it's colder than a…" A car passed in the street, and Bee stiffened. It turned off before it reached us, thankfully. "We'd better make this quick, Rubes. Let's go." She gestured to the gate.

"What? Me? First?"

"Yes, you first. You've got the younger legs."

"Only by twenty-odd years."

She wrinkled her nose at me.

"All right, all right." I glanced left and right down the street then hurried to the gate. I closed my gloves around the metal spokes, and the cold came through, regardless of the comfy sheep's wool lining. I found a spot for my foot then climbed over, avoiding the spikes at the top. I dropped down on the other side. "See? Easy."

"You did make that look elegant," Bee said, tugging down the corners of her black beanie. "All right. I'm coming over." Bee was skinny and all arms and legs as she scrambled over the gate. She dropped down beside me, dusting off her gloves. "Easy peasy lemon squeezy."

"Ten out of ten."

Bee affected a gymnast's landing pose. "Why, thank you. Now," she said, her expression growing serious, "let's find out what we're dealing with here before spooky church ghosts come to get us." Bee switched on the flashlight she'd brought with her and directed it over the snow. "This way."

"Wait," I said, catching her arm before she could move off. "Look." I nodded to the wall.

Snow had fallen during the day, and the layer on the ground near the wall and leading back toward the church was disturbed by a set of footsteps leading to and from it. The trail stopped next to the brick wall, right where Misty had pointed out the mystery watcher.

The beam from the flashlight slashed across the white snow. "What's that?" Bee asked.

I crossed to the prints, careful not to disturb them, and Bee joined me, crouching over.

"It's dust," I whispered, pointing toward the base of the wall. "How odd. Look. The footsteps come from the back of the church."

Bee directed the light along the footprints toward the back of the church. They ended at the door. "Yeah, and to this wall." Bee pointed the flashlight to where the footsteps had stopped. "That looks like... brick dust?" She gestured to the dust next to the two steps imprinted in the snow. "Which could mean that they, what, climbed over?"

"And then over again to walk back through the church? Why?" I frowned.

"Perhaps they gripped the wall so hard that they scraped off some dust?" Bee feathered the flashlight's beam over the spot where the stone met the wrought iron spikes. "Nothing. Puzzling. That's very puzzling."

"Wait a second... Bee! The snow only fell today. That means that these are fresh sets of tracks. Someone came here days after the mayor's murder," I hissed.

A car turned into the street adjacent to the church's yard, and Bee clicked off her flashlight, plunging us into darkness. We ducked low beneath the stone portion of the wall, waiting for it to move on.

"What do you think?" I whispered.

"That someone came back here to check out the crime scene after the fact."

"That or it's just a groundskeeper."

"A groundskeeper who walks a selected route to the back wall of the church and nowhere else?" The passing car's headlights lit up the churchyard a little, and Bee's frown was clearer. "This is very strange."

"What does this mean? That we have to find someone with brick dust on their shoes?"

The car swept off, and we were left in darkness again.

"It means," Bee said, "that we—"

A creaking from the back of the church interrupted her.

Bee and I turned toward the noise. A darkened figure wearing a hoodie stood on the back steps, watching us.

Eleven

"Bee," I whispered. "Are you seeing what I'm seeing?"

"You mean the ghostly figure watching us from the back of the church?"

"I was thinking more like the creepy person watching us from the back of the church."

"To-may-to, to-mah-to," Bee replied.

"Bee. He's moving." Assuming it was a he, the figure on the back step of the church was, indeed, approaching. One purposeful step at a time, walking almost as though we were animals who could be scared off by sudden movements.

"Oh my heavens," Bee said. "I think you're right."

"What do we do?" It was possibly the dumbest question that had ever left my lips—obviously we had to run—but I could barely think straight. Panic trickled down my spine. *It's got to be the killer. They've come back to the scene of the crime.*

Something glinted in the figure's hand, and I sucked in a breath.

"We fight," Bee said. "Come on, Ruby. We can take them down. There's two of us and only one of them."

"That would be great," I whispered, squeaking it out and backing away, "like a really great idea if they weren't holding a gun or knife in their hand, right now."

Bee froze. "Oh. That's regrettable."

"Regrettable? More like terrifying."

"Fine. Terrifying. But I still think that—"

The figure grunted and quickened their pace, crunching across the snow toward us. Our time for cute conversation was up.

"Run!" I cried and scrambled toward the gate. I was up and over in two seconds flat, but Bee had gotten the back of her jeans caught on the spikes.

"Help," she said. "Help, help. I'm stuck." She stretched out her arms, and I grabbed hold of them and pulled with all my might. The figure stormed toward us, and a shriek got stuck in my throat.

"Pull harder!" Bee yelled, glancing over her shoulder,

her legs kicking against the bottom of the gate and clanging loudly. "Quick!" She was suspended half-way up, her beanie askew on her head. "Ruby!"

I gave a massive tug.

There was a terrific *riiip* of fabric, and Bee screeched and fell free of the gate. She landed majestically a second time, on her high-heeled boots with poise. No gymnast poses, though, as Bee sprinted off, and I followed, darting after her down the sidewalk, a fine layer of snow falling in front of us.

"I lost my flashlight," Bee panted. "He's got my flashlight!"

"I think we've got bigger problems right now. Better that he has your flashlight than our lives." I glanced over my shoulder, but the figure hadn't climbed the church fence yet. "We've got to—"

"Watch out!" Bee yelled.

I skidded to a halt, but it was too late. I careened directly into something warm and slightly squishy.

"Ow!" It was a person. A woman.

I caught her arms, before we could both fall to the slippery wet ground, and tried steadying myself. My boots slid, and I ran on the spot, bobbling left and right, until, finally, Bee grabbed me from behind and held me in place.

"Relax, Michael Flatley," she said.

"Very funny."

"Not funny at all!" Ava Jacobsen, the mayor's grieving window, tugged her arms from my grasp and glared at me through narrowed green eyes. She wore a puffy black jacket and a pair of jeans, her blonde hair tied up in a severe bun. She lifted a Kleenex to the end of her nose and sniffed. "You nearly knocked me over. What on earth are you two doing running around at this time of night?"

"It's seven pm," I said, trying not to take the scolding to heart.

"And we could ask you the same question, Mrs. Jacobsen." Bee's tone was sharper than Ava's had been.

What *was* she doing on this street, so close to the Christmas tree where her husband's body had been found? Wasn't it true that the murderer always returned to the scene of the crime? Or was that just a movie thing?

"If you must know, I was out for a walk. I thought of doing Christmas shopping, but it was too difficult. Who am I going to shop for?" Ava's last sentence came out as a cry, but Bee didn't seem affected by it.

"Sorry for nearly knocking you over," I said. "We just, uh, we wanted to get back to the Oceanside. We don't want to miss Shawn's fantastic dinner."

"Right." Bee lifted a black-gloved hand. "I heard he's making a roast chicken tonight. With crispy potatoes and lemon-butter sauce."

"Lemon-butter without fish?" Ava's upper lip pulled back. "How strange."

It boded well for us that Ava found the lemon-butter sauce with chicken stranger than she found us in our all-black getups. I shivered and rubbed my arms. "We'd better get back to the guesthouse," I said. "Are you, uh, coming, Ava?"

"Me?" Ava's gaze darted past us and up the street. Toward the church? Or the tree? "Oh, well, sure, yeah. I guess I should head back. It's cold, and I *am* hungry. This shopping thing was a bad idea."

Shopping, huh? But most of the places in Carmel Springs had already closed. Besides, there wasn't much to buy from the General Store. Most folks shopped for Christmas presents online and had them delivered.

What exactly was Ava hiding?

"All right," I said. "Let's get you back to the Oceanside."

"Yeah." Bee gave me a knowing look. "A person could catch their death out here."

Ava sobbed.

"Poor choice of words, Bee," I whispered, as I tucked my arm around Ava's shoulders and guided her down the street. Ava was reluctant. She paused again, turning toward the tree then shaking her head and muttering under her breath. She dabbed under her eyes with a crumpled Kleenex.

"I wish things were different," Ava said.

I couldn't help but wonder, different how? And what exactly had Ava been doing out here at this time of the evening and in this icy weather?

Twelve

The minute we arrived back at the Oceanside Guesthouse, Ava started off up the stairs with a vague murmur about having an early night. I wasn't about to stop her, though Bee looked as if she might. Regardless, I was frozen to the core.

I had food and hot cocoa and a stint by the fire on my mind. Questioning Ava could wait. Likely, it wouldn't yield much even if we did question her now. Ava was either shaken up or shutting down.

"Hello!" Sam popped up from behind the reception desk, her hair tied neatly and a smattering of lip gloss on her lips. How strange—Sam had never been big on makeup.

It's Detective Martin. She's dating him, remember?

"Hi," I said, through chattering teeth.

"Why are you two dressed like spies?" Sam asked.

Bee's eyes widened. She removed her beanie and black gloves hurriedly. "We're just wearing jeans and black jackets," she said.

"And gloves and beanies," Sam noted. "Is everything OK?"

"Of course," I said. "We were wearing black... in honor of Mayor Jacobsen." It was technically true—we'd donned the nightly colors so that we could solve his murder mystery. That counted as honoring him, didn't it?

"Oh, right. Poor Ian." Sam peered over at the stairs to the second floor. "And poor Ava," she whispered. "She hasn't been right ever since it happened. She's all over the place. I heard her talking to herself in her room last night."

"Goodness," Bee said. "That *is* sad."

I got the distinct impression that Bee had wanted to say "interesting" instead of "sad." "Did you overhear what she was saying? Maybe she was on the phone."

"Maybe." Sam shrugged. "She was crying quite heavily, though, and saying 'no' a lot. Anyway." Sam shuddered. "I'm sure we've all had enough sorrow for today. Why don't you lovely ladies go through to the living room? Shawn's almost finished preparing dinner. Roast chicken."

"Delish," Bee said.

We hurried into the living room and found our favorite spots in front of the fire empty. Well, apart from

Trouble, who had taken up residence on one of the armchairs. I lifted the calico kitty and sat down, placing him on my lap.

Trouble arched his back and gave a big ol' yawn, then settled down again, purring and kneading my cold jeans.

"That's so much better," I said.

Bee fluffed her hair then placed her palms out toward the fire. "You can say that again. Nothing like a jaunt through a creepy churchyard to get ice in the veins."

"That church's yard wasn't creepy. It was the—"

Sam bustled into the living room, smiling as if she had a happy secret. "Would you like some hot cocoa? I'm about to fix myself some, and I've got a batch of delicious gingerbread men fresh out of the oven. Shawn is such a treasure."

"Yes, please. That would be amazing," I said.

Sam hurried off into the kitchen, the door, with its porthole window, swinging closed after her. She was back a few minutes later with the steaming cups of cocoa, mini-marshmallows bobbing in the mugs.

"Perfect," I said. "Thank you so much, Sam."

"Sit with us, please." Bee gestured to the last armchair. "It's so warm by the fire."

Sam took a place and sipped on her cocoa, her eyes sparkling and focused on the flames. "What a strange time this is," she said. "The murder of the mayor, right around

Christmas. I don't know who would do something like this."

"We have a few suspects," Bee said.

I shot a look her way, but she patted the air.

We'd never kept anything from Sam before, not really, but now that she was dating the lead detective on the murder case, things had changed. If Sam told Martin we'd decided to look into it, he'd take action against us. He'd warned us this afternoon that interfering would only lead to trouble.

And not the furry, purring kind.

"Suspects?" Sam set her cocoa mug down and shifted in her seat. "So, you two are looking into it again?"

"It depends," Bee said.

"On what?"

"On whether you're going to tell Detective Martin that we're interested."

Sam nibbled on her lower lip. "No, I wouldn't do that. I like Frank a lot, but I wouldn't get you two in trouble because of that. Besides, you've helped me so much with the Oceanside. You introduced me to Shawn, and when Detective Jones died—"

"Right," Bee said. "Then we can trust you."

"Of course."

Bee and I gave each other another glance—we'd gotten better at reading each other. It was all the baking and solving crimes. I'd never had as close of a friend as Beatrice.

"We just ran into Ava near the Christmas tree in the center of town," I said, as quietly as I could. "Naturally, as the spouse of the deceased, she's a person of interest."

"To us. We don't know what's going on with the police investigation," Bee put in.

"Exactly. Though, we did see Detective Martin talking to Greta Gould on the pier the other day."

Sam's lips drew into a thin line at Greta's name. "That woman," she said, "is a scourge. She's so full of herself."

"We've noticed," I said.

"She's been giving poor Frankie so much trouble," Sam continued. "He tried bringing her in for questioning for involvement in the case, but she called a lawyer before he could do a thing. Now she's refusing to talk."

"He told you all of this?" Bee asked, incredulous.

"Well, yes. He's been stressed lately, you know. This is the first time he's been the lead detective on a case like this, apart from when Jones was murdered, and it seems like he doesn't have much by way of evidence. He needed someone to talk to." Sam lifted her mug and hid her lips behind it. "I really shouldn't have said anything."

"It's OK," I said. "We won't tell anyone."

"I mean we should," Bee grumbled. "That's highly inappropriate behavior from a detective. It's not like the case details have been released on Discovery. This is an ongoing investigation." As an ex-cop, Bee was bound to get annoyed about shoddy police work.

"She's kidding." I leaned over slightly, careful not to disturb Trouble in my lap, and patted Sam on the arm. "Everything will be fine. I'm sure the murder will be solved soon. OK?"

"I guess."

The kitchen doors opened, and Shawn appeared wearing, of all things, an ugly Christmas sweater complete with white bobbles and a reindeer knitted on the front. Shawn was into the goth style of living, with dark hair and eye makeup. He flicked that hair back now and crooked a finger in Sam's direction. "Dinner's ready, boss."

"Coming!" Sam practically jumped and sloshed a little cocoa over her legs. She giggled nervously then darted off toward the doors.

"Hmm." Bee tapped the tip of her nose. "Now, that's interesting."

"Seems like Greta's involved somehow. But why? And how?"

"I think it's time we pay a visit to the mayor's offices," Bee said. "If Greta was there, someone's bound to remember her. She's not exactly inconspicuous."

We had our next lead. The plot had thickened. Hopefully, the lemon-butter sauce for the roast chicken hadn't.

Thirteen

Carmel Springs' mayor's office was situated in a double story building off Main Street. The outside was painted a murky brown, but the glass front door was clean and dust-free.

"Do you really think we're going to find out anything of use?" I asked.

"Of course," Bee replied. "With my superior investigative skills and your emotional tact, we're bound to get to the bottom of this."

I followed Bee into the mayor's offices, removing my gloves. The thermostat was set way too high in here, and I pulled off my jacket too and hung it up on a stand near the door. Bee did the same, brushing her hair back from her forehead and casting that sharp-eyed gaze around the place.

The reception desk, right near another door that led to the offices, was manned by a young woman with flyaway dark hair and a bulbous nose. She picked at her lips and turned the pages in a magazine, the tips of her scuffed shoes poking out from under the desk to greet us.

"Good morning," I said.

The woman screamed.

Bee stiffened. I jolted back a step.

"Oh, sorry," she said and laughed hysterically, still picking her lips. "I've been a little bit on edge ever since... you know, the mayor was strangled to death with a string of lights."

"Right," I said. "Of course."

"Definitely a reason to scream at passersby," Bee muttered.

"So, what can I help you with?" the receptionist asked, tucking a finger between the pages of her magazine and closing it. "Do you want to speak to a—"

The door behind her opened, and the mayor's assistant, Jerry Flagg, stepped out. "Is everything OK, Cheryl?"

"Just me again," the receptionist said, with another maniacal laugh. "You know how on edge I've been ever since... the mayor was strangled with a string of lights."

"She just said that the exact same way," Bee whispered. "How strange."

Jerry looked up and spotted us. His expression lightened from concern to happiness. "Hello, ladies. It's great to see you again." He reached back and tightened his ponytail. "I'm so sorry about your Christmas party. I was hoping that the good detective would lift the embargo on all things fun, but no dice."

"He's not interested?"

"Nope. He says his hands are tied. The town council wants to keep everyone safe." Jerry rolled his eyes. "Seems to me like the mayor's murder was personal. I don't see why they'd be worried about some serial killer on the loose."

Cheryl gasped, and the lip-picking intensified.

"Sorry," Jerry said and patted her awkwardly on the shoulder. "Would you like to come through and talk to someone?"

"Actually," I said, shifting my weight from one foot to the other. "We wanted to talk to you."

"Yes, about the celebration."

"Oh, of course," Jerry said. "Right this way."

We followed him past panicky Cheryl and down a short hall past a few cubicles. "The mayor's personal office is on the floor above this," Jerry said. "He wouldn't have been caught dead down here with us."

The place was pretty empty, likely because it was so

close to Christmas, and because, well, folks were scared after the murder.

"Here," Jerry said, opening a door to a small room. It contained a desk, a potted plant that had probably died two months ago, and an old air-conditioning unit with rust creeping down its side. He gestured to the rickety chairs in front of the desk and took a seat behind it.

Bee and I sat, and I pressed my hands together in my lap. Why was I so nervous? This wasn't a big deal. I'd interviewed loads of people before, and it had never bothered me.

"We were wondering what your thoughts are on getting the council to let us have the party." It was the first thing that had popped into mind, and I pulled on the thread harder. "Do you think there's any way we could convince them to lift the ban for one night? Everyone's already got their invites."

"I'm not sure about that," Jerry said, sitting back and fiddling with his golden hoop earring. "Convincing them might be tough. They're a bunch of old fogies. The type that don't care much for change."

"Fogies," Bee said, narrowing her eyes at him.

"Oh, no offense."

"Why would I take offense?" Bee asked. "Are you saying I'm old?"

"Uh..."

"Maybe," I said, saving Jerry before Bee's wrath unseated our investigation, "maybe we could get someone influential to help us out. Do you know anyone like that?"

Jerry rocked back and forth, considering it.

"What about Greta Gould?" Bee prompted, helping out with the thread-pulling. "I heard she's buying the paper."

"Oh, that's right," Jerry said, pointing at Bee. "You're onto something there. She's also been around here a lot too."

"What? At the mayor's office?"

"Oh yeah," Jerry said. "She often called Mayor Jacobsen. They would spend hours on the phone talking about things."

"What things?" Bee asked.

"Oh, I don't know for sure. Some of it was good and some of it annoyed the mayor. He used to walk around complaining about how that Gould woman couldn't stop putting her over-sized nose where it didn't belong. Really got under his skin."

"Hmm." Bee tapped her chin.

"Maybe," I said, "we could talk to her about the whole council-party thing. What do you think?"

"That's a great idea. I'll tell you, we need some fun in this town. I could call her for you if you like."

"No," I said, quickly, then measured my tone. "No, that's fine. You've done enough, Jerry, thank you. We'd like to talk to her in person. Convince her, you know?"

"Right, sure. Well, she's staying in the Cove at the Clover Pot Hotel," he said.

The Cove was near the other end of Carmel Springs and was more out of the town than in it. The Clover Pot was Sam's only competition, except it wasn't really, because it was overdone, too expensive, and too far out of the way for most folks who came to town.

"Then we have our next step," Bee said. "Thanks for your time, Mr. Flagg."

"Please, call me Jerry." He got up and we followed suite. He shook my hand then Bee's, and I cast a quick glance at his shoes, just in case. They were plain and black, a little scuffed, but without brick dust in sight.

Of course there wouldn't be. It wasn't like brick dust just clung to shoes forever. A ridiculous thought. But still, it was good to get into the habit of studying people if we were to solve the murder.

"Thanks for your time, Jerry," I said.

"Let me know what Greta says." He walked us out.

Cheryl had resumed reading the magazine at the reception desk and managed not to scream as we gathered our coats and exited into the street. The town's lampposts had been decorated with fairy lights, but I wasn't feeling the festive vibe now.

"To the Clover Pot Hotel," I said. "And step on it."

"Step on what? We're not in the food truck," Bee said, as we headed back down the road to where we'd parked.

"Sheesh, can a woman use a cool line once in a while?"

Fourteen

"WHY DO YOU THINK SHE CHOSE THE CLOVER Pot?" I steered the food truck down the road, carefully, past the soup kitchen and toward the Cove. "Why not just stay at the Oceanside?" Sam's establishment was more popular than the Clover Pot, and for good reason. She provided a homely feel and amazing food. There were always interesting folks to talk to. That was the beauty of a guesthouse.

Whereas the Clover Pot was professional, removed. They probably had a breakfast or restaurant option, but there was no sense of community. It was just a hotel.

"She doesn't want to be noticed," Bee said. "That or she's rich enough to rent a big suite for an extended period of time."

"I wonder why she doesn't have a place of her own here. Is she an out-of-towner?"

"I'm not sure. We could ask Millie. And if she is from somewhere else, why's she interested in investing in the paper?"

"And what was she doing in the butchery the other day?" I added in. "She surely didn't need a turkey. Where would she cook it?"

"Let's find out."

I pulled into a parking space in front of the Clover Pot Hotel and peered up at it. It was a three-story, with a largely empty parking lot out front and decorated for glitz and glamor. The hotel bore a wide porch and two marble pillars either side of its front door. Its back had a view of the cove and the now-icy deep blue waters and the rocks below.

The hotel itself didn't fit in with the aesthetic of Carmel Springs.

"Bit of an eyesore if you ask me," Bee said.

"Ostentatious."

"Exactly."

Bee and I hurried from the truck, bracing ourselves against the wind, and into the reception area. It was magnificent, with marble floors and a central chandelier full of glittering crystals. The woman behind the desk wore a neat uniform and a fake smile.

"Welcome to the Clover Pot Hotel," she said. "How may I help you today?"

"Hi," I said, slightly taken aback by her super cheery attitude. "We're here to see Ms. Gould? Greta Gould?"

"Oh. Do you have an appointment with her?" The receptionist blinked, tilting her head to one side.

"Uh…"

"Yes, yes we do," Bee put in. "We're from the local paper. We'd like to talk to her about her acquisition of it and plans for the future." It was a neat little lie.

I gave Bee an appraising look, and she winked at me when the receptionist wasn't looking.

"I'm sorry," the uniformed woman said, holding the phone to her chest, "it appears that Ms. Gould isn't in her room."

"Oh. Oh all right," I said. "We'll come back later."

Bee and I thanked the receptionist and made our way across the marble hall and out onto the front steps. The food truck waited beneath the overcast sky, and so did another car—a shining black Corvette. The doors were open, and two people stood in front of the tapered hood.

Greta and the Babcock.

Bee stopped dead in her tracks.

I did too.

"What's that about?" I whispered.

Bee tugged on my arm, looped hers through it, then walked us down the steps and toward the sports car.

Greta and the Babcock stopped talking immediately. Greta tossed her long golden-red hair back, and the Babcock put up a cheesy smile that would've looked perfectly at home at a bad actors' convention.

"Good morning," I said, as we came down the steps.

"Hello." Greta folded her arms. "What are you doing here?"

"We were thinking of moving from the Oceanside to the Clover Pot," I said.

Good heavens, I wasn't a fan of lying, but I'd become adept at telling these fibs. It was shameful. It would also help us figure out who'd killed the mayor. Hopefully.

"You." Greta raised a perfectly plucked eyebrow. "Here?"

"Yes," Bee replied, drawing herself up straight. "We were looking for a classier establishment."

"Well, I don't blame you," the Babcock said, in his booming "listen to me, everybody" voice. "That Oceanside is so run down. Really, who would want to stay in such a small, rickety old place when there's the Clover Pot Hotel out here? It's beyond reason."

"You're the butcher, right?" I asked.

"Clayton Babcock," he simpered, sticking out a hand. "Such a pleasure to meet you. I was just having a quick chat with my dear friend Greta over here about your food truck." He gestured. "I heard you're serving delicious treats."

"When it's not so icy cold we are," I said, shaking his hand. *His dear friend Greta? Why would the butcher and this strange golden-haired mogul be friends?*

"Well, I think that's great," Babcock continued. "I think that if we..." He continued talking, but my mind flittered elsewhere, all while I nodded along. Why on earth were the butcher and the Broadway-star-wannabe out here talking? I didn't buy it had been about the food truck.

They'd clearly arrived in the fancy black Corvette together. Which meant they were definitely friends. Or having an affair? But did that have anything to do with Mayor Jacobsen's death?

Bee nudged me, ever so gently, and I found her staring downward at the sidewalk. No! At the Babcock's shoes. They bore a fine layer of... what was that? Brick dust? It was reddish and sort of clumpy, molded to the outsides of his black boots. Perhaps he'd walked through some snow and managed to paste the brick dust to the fronts of his shoes.

My eyes widened.

"What?" Greta snapped. "What are you staring at the ground like that for?"

"Oh! Sorry," I managed. "I was just, uh, thinking

about all the things I had to do today. Christmas is such a busy time, isn't it Bee?"

"Busy like a bee," she said and gave an awkward chuckle.

"It was lovely seeing you again, Ms. Gould," I said. "Good luck with the acquisition of the paper." Poor Millie. I couldn't imagine working for a woman like Greta. But, hopefully, if she turned out to be the killer, we could lock her away for good. "And it was great to meet you too, Mr. Babcock."

"Yes, of course, of course," he blustered, offering us another cheesy smile.

I rushed to the food truck, and we slipped into the cab and put on our seat belts. Bee let out a breath and erected a fake smile of her own. "Pretend to be laughing and joking about something," she said. "Greta's watching."

I faked a laugh and glanced, briefly, over at the Corvette. Greta stood twirling a strand of hair around her gloved finger, glaring at the truck. The Babcock was oblivious to Greta's lack of interest in his story.

"Let's get out of here," Bee said, with a pronounced giggle. "You know, before she burns a hole in the side of the truck with her glare."

I reversed out of the parking spot and put distance between us and Greta Gould.

"Did you see it?" I asked. "Did you see the shoes?"

"Brick dust. Pasted up brick dust. I'm sure of it. And do you know what that means?" Bee turned in the comfy passenger seat, the fabric scraping beneath her thick coat.

"What?"

"It's time for another stakeout!"

I groaned. The last stakeout had been beyond uncomfortable. And they seemed to be Bee's favorite thing to do.

"Don't take that attitude, Rubes," Bee said, slapping the back of her hand against her palm. "Stakeouts are an integral part of any good investigation. This means that we're closer than ever to solving the crime."

"I hope you're right." But something told me there was more to Greta Gould than met the eye.

Fifteen

There were two major problems with staking out the butchery. Firstly, our food truck wasn't inconspicuous. The pink and green pastel stripes stood out against the white snow. And secondly, being out on the street without the food truck was both icy and suspicious in itself. Nobody was out hanging around the fronts of stores or buildings in this weather. The minute they arrived at their destinations, they all rushed right inside.

As a result, Bee and I had opted for the first impossible stakeout option. We sat in the front of the food truck across from the butcher's pretending that everything was fine and it wasn't completely obvious that we were just hanging around.

"Well, this is embarrassing," I muttered, as yet another

person walked by and frowned at us, puzzled by our presence.

We'd already had three people knocking on the windows asking if we'd open anytime soon and had to tell them we were closed for Christmas. That only drew more frowns and questions.

"Don't worry, we're fine," Bee said. "We're hiding in plain sight."

"Bee, it doesn't feel like we're hiding much at all. I'm sure Babcock knows we're here."

"Oh, don't be so certain." Bee nodded to the butchery. Inside it Babcock stood behind the counter talking enthusiastically with his customers. A half an hour earlier, he'd leaped onto the counter again and likely gone into another "save Carmel Springs" rant. "The man is oblivious to anything that doesn't fit into stroking his ego."

I had to admit, she had a point. The Babcock wore his butcher's apron like it was a coat made of medallions and proclaimed his true worth. He grinned and spread his arms, welcoming people to the butchery like they'd stepped into his palace.

"All right," I said. "So maybe he hasn't noticed us. But nothing's happening either. He's just hanging around in the shop, talking about..."

"How great he is as a mayoral candidate?"

"Probably," I said. "What if he—" I cut off.

The Babcock had slipped out from behind the counter at the back of his shop. He took off his apron and withdrew a phone from his pocket then waved to the customers and held up a finger. He exited the butchery and tramped around the side of it and into the alleyway.

"Well, would you look at that," I breathed.

"Follow him, quick."

"What, in the food truck? I don't think we'll fit into the alley—"

"Rubes!" Bee had already unclipped her seatbelt and opened her door.

"Right. Of course."

We darted across the street, definitely not nonchalant in the slightest, and stood near the mouth to the alleyway. He wasn't in it. But the Babcock's sonorous voice traveled from somewhere around the back of the building.

"—telling you."

Bee gestured toward the other end of the alley, where there was a corner, likely one that looked on the back of the butchery, and set off toward it.

My heart did a flip. What if the Babcock caught us? What if he was the real murderer?

I shoved the thoughts aside. This was a lead. A real one. I stopped behind Bee at the corner, and we both peered around it and caught sight of the Babcock.

He stood in the center of the breezeway, between

bricks that had been scattered messily across the concrete. There was brick dust here, there, and everywhere. The wall itself had collapsed, and on the other side of it stood a scaffold and what looked like the long-abandoned remnants of a construction in progress.

My stomach sank.

Brick dust?

Then there was no proof that the brick dust on Babcock's shoes had come from the churchyard. Instead, it had most definitely come from here.

"I want this worked out, Greta," he said.

I stiffened. Greta? Maybe this stakeout would give us some useful information. Just how close were the unlikely friends? Close enough to commit murder together? After all, we had no proof that the person who'd been in the churchyard was the murderer.

"No, no, no. It's unacceptable. They knocked down my back wall, and they haven't been back to fix it for over a week," he said then paused and listened to what Greta had to say. "I don't care if it's Christmas. I'm working, and it's Christ—" He pursed his lips, shaking his head furiously. "No, *you* don't understand. You told me you wanted to invest in my campaign, and you did. This is a part of that. What if people notice the mess at my butchery? They'll assume I'm not capable of managing anything. Then they won't vote me in."

Greta's an investor? A campaign investor?

Shock guttered through me.

Of course! That would give her a direct reason to get rid of Mayor Jacobsen. The Babcock had run against him and had lost in November. Likely, Greta had wanted to take control of the town and use the butcher as a puppet.

After all, wasn't she taking control of the paper? She wanted to use it to get her message out as well. It was a power play.

"No, Greta. It's important. If we want to win the town over, everything we do has to be immaculate. And if my butchery doesn't fit that aesthetic, then how do you expect me to win?" The Babcock turned around and paced to the other end of the space, his voice fading.

My thoughts whirred, but Bee placed a hand on my arm and stopped them. She squeezed, and we slowly backed out of the alley and back into the—

"Oof!" I struck something solid behind us.

Oh no. My insides mushed into jelly, and my cheeks flushed hot. I didn't have to look over at Bee to know the same had happened to her.

Because it wasn't a wall I'd walked into. It was Detective Martin.

Sixteen

Detective Martin adjusted his beanie, glaring at us and channeling the anger his old partner, Jones, had always had when it came to Bee and me. "What do we have here? Out for a stroll, ladies?"

"Good morning, detective," I squeaked. "We were just—"

"Snooping."

"No, um..."

"There's no point in denying it," Martin said, running a gloved hand over his stubbly chin. "I watched Mr. Babcock enter the alleyway way and you follow him."

Well, darn. How were we supposed to get out of this one? "We were just, um, going to ask him about our turkey order," I said.

"Yeah." Bee snapped her fingers. "Our turkey order.

We ordered a turkey from the butchery for the Oceanside's Christmas feast, and it hasn't been delivered yet."

Martin looked on the brink of rolling his eyes at us. "Ladies, you and I both know that's not true. Now, I'm not here to lock you away for interfering. I was at the Oceanside a half an hour ago looking for you, and Sam told me that you'd be out here."

"Oh." Of course she'd told him. They were dating now. And we hadn't made it a secret that we'd be in town, hanging around.

"Your food truck is parked across from the butchery, but you're not open for business," Martin continued, "so please don't insult my intelligence by trying to squirm out of this one."

"Fine," I said, though Bee shook her head at me. "Fine, we were just here because we wanted to find out more about him. He's suspicious. He has a motive for the murder, and his partner and friend, Greta is—"

The detective lifted a hand. "That's enough," he said. "There's no reason for you to be checking this out. There never was. But particularly not now."

"Why?" Bee asked.

And why had he been looking for us in the first place? It wasn't as if we'd done anything illegal, that he knew of. Sheesh, what had I become? Flouting the laws because I was desperate to uncover the truth about the murder.

"Because the murderer has already been apprehended," Martin said.

I sucked in a breath. "What? How is that possible?"

"Contrary to your beliefs, Miss Holmes, the Carmel Springs Police Department is capable of solving crimes. Even ones as severe as this one."

"I didn't say you weren't capable." But I'd thought we were stumped, so surely the police had to be.

"Who is it?" Bee asked.

Detective Martin drew his lips into a thin line. Apparently, releasing that information to us, even now, bit at him. He'd changed since Jones's death. He was still handsome and tall, but he looked a lot older, as if the strain of running things had taken its toll.

"Ava Jacobsen."

"What?" Bee gasped.

"No. It can't be," I said. "She didn't have a motive. And she was right there in the crowd before the tree lighting. And she was so upset." Of course, we had suspected her at first, but none of our leads had brought us closer toward her as a person of interest.

"Well, it is."

"How did you come to that conclusion?" I asked.

Detective Martin sighed. "Look, I'm not obligated to answer any questions, but I know you two will keep poking around if I don't tell you the truth. Ava's fingerprints were found on the murder weapon."

"What, the string of lights?" I asked. "But surely you must have found other prints. I mean, isn't it possible that—?"

"Trust that the police know what they're doing, Holmes," Martin said, stiffly. "The murder investigation is closed. If you have any complaints... well, shelve them."

My jaw dropped. The detective had never been this blunt before.

"Which brings me to my next piece of news," he said. "Your Christmas party is back on."

"Really? The town's open again? For celebration and caroling?" I asked.

"Correct. Now why don't you two get back in your food truck and go to the Oceanside? It's been a long morning, and I don't want to have to throw you in jail for trespassing or stalking. All right?"

Bee was so red in the face she looked ready to pop, but it wasn't from embarrassment. She fumed. And I did too. The whole Ava thing didn't make sense to me.

"Go on," Detective said, gesturing back toward the truck.

"You can't just tell us to leave like that." But Bee started off across the street regardless. The minute we were out of earshot, the grumbling started. "That man! I can't believe he thinks he's so smart. I don't buy this for a second, Ruby. They're missing crucial evidence, I'm sure of it."

"But we do get to do the party, at least." It was my effort at cheering her up.

We got into the food truck and buckled ourselves in.

"What do you think?" Bee asked. "That he's right?"

"No. I don't know." I drummed my fingertips on the steering wheel. "But I do think there's something we can do to find out."

"What?" Bee asked.

"Go see Ava in jail. I mean, she's surely allowed to have a visitor or two, right? So, let's go talk to her and hear her side of the story. If she did it, then we can just let it go. The case will be solved, and we can focus on setting up for the party and celebrating Christmas with our friends."

"But what if it's not?" Bee asked, her silvery eyebrows two slashes above her hazel gaze.

"Then we do what we've always done with this type of thing. We investigate." I'd been dubious about doing exactly that, but it was clear to me now that there was more to be uncovered.

If Detective Martin refused to see it, it was up to us to get to the bottom of the mystery.

Even if that meant getting in trouble again. And possibly ruining Christmas.

Seventeen

AVA WAS FORCED TO WEAR HANDCUFFS AS SHE sat across from us in the tiny visitors' room at the police station. The room itself was well-lit, with chairs that weren't exactly comfy but were fine and a melamine-topped table holding three bottles of water.

The fact that we weren't on a visitors list hadn't been a problem, simply because Ava hadn't been transferred to an actual prison yet. She was still in the holding cells at the station itself. I didn't doubt there were cameras all over the place in here.

That was fine.

If Ava had done it and admitted it, no problem. And if she hadn't... well, hopefully she'd give us some clue as to who might have.

"I can't thank you enough for coming to see me," Ava

said, her eyes bloodshot and her cheeks splotchy. Her blonde hair was tied back but hadn't been washed in a few days. They'd only arrested Ava that morning, but she hadn't been looking after herself.

Who could blame her?

Maybe she did do it.

What an awful thought to have. But it was a possibility. I had to bear that in mind. It wouldn't help the investigation if I went in biased.

Ava shifted under the scrutiny from Bee—my bestie in baking sat on the seat next to mine, making direct eye contact with the suspected murderess. Not, suspected, now, but accused.

"How are you, Ava?" I asked, to distract from Bee's glare.

"I've been better," Ava whispered, choking it out. "I'm grateful I have visitors, but it's been such a difficult time. I don't know how I'm going to handle everything. I mean, I have money for a lawyer, but this is just... I would never have hurt Ian. He was the love of my life."

There were no tears, and the way she spoke was ever-so-slightly mechanical. Like she was sure she had to say that. How strange.

"Listen, why would I have murdered him?" Ava asked, shifting to the edge of her seat. "And if I had, why would I have been so upset that I moved out of the house? I loved my husband." Once again, every word sounded right, but the way they were delivered was empty.

None of the sorrow that had been there at the beginning of the week was present. Had she been faking it before?

"And now," Ava said, letting out a choice sniffle, "now everyone's going to think that I'm a terrible person." Her voice cracked, and she finally showed a few tears. "But I'm not. I wouldn't hurt a fly. I can imagine that it's going to be so difficult going forward. People will judge me. I'll get hate mail. I'll..."

"You're sure you had no part in this?" Bee asked, gruffly.

"Of course not," Ava said, in a low whine. "I would never. Look, please, I know you two are good at investigating these types of things. Can you help me? Please?"

"Help you how?" Bee asked.

"Clear my name."

Bee and I exchanged a glance. We'd come here under the impression that Ava was innocent, but now I wasn't so sure. What if we helped and somehow got her out of prison when she was the culprit? But no, that wasn't right. We'd only wind up finding the truth.

"We might be able to help you," I said, after a moment. "Do you have any idea who might have wanted to do something like this to your husband?"

"Yes," Ava hissed. "I know exactly who did it."

"You do?"

"Yes, absolutely. It was Clayton Babcock," she replied. "I mentioned him before, remember? I'm convinced now. He was out for blood after my husband won the election. And I just know he had access to the staging area for the tree-lighting ceremony. And he would've had access to the strings of lights." Ava shook her head. "Ian was the one who brought all the lights from home to give to the tree. That's why my fingerprints were on it. That's the only reason."

"You really believe that Clayton did this?" I asked.

"Yes, totally. He was in a rage after my husband won. He even closed down the butchery for a whole day. There was an uproar afterward. There was almost a riot."

We'd been in Carmel Springs in November, and I didn't remember any riot. "Are people that desperate for meat?"

"You bet they are. Especially around this time of year," Ava said.

"I don't remember any riot." Bee folded her arms. "Are you sure about that?"

"Positive. And the Babcock was Ian's sworn enemy. Surely, you've heard that?"

"Yes, that I've heard," I said.

"Well there you have it," Ava replied. "He's the one

who did it. Trust me. Look, all you'd have to do is follow him around, and you'll find out the truth. Trust me."

She'd said to trust her twice. That didn't implicitly instill much trust in me.

"Please," Ava said, her bottom lip quivering. "You've got to get me out of here. I don't want to go to prison."

What about finding your husband's killer? Doesn't that matter?

"We'll do what we can," Bee said, after a second. "But if you know anything else, you have to tell us. Otherwise we can't help."

"I don't know anything else. It was Clayton. That's all I can tell you. It was definitely Clayton. He used to get into fights with Ian. He would call the office and leave snarky messages. I'm sure you can get hold of them. Maybe that can be the evidence you need." The words rolled from her tongue. "What do you think? Can you bring him down?"

"We'll get to the bottom of this," I said, slowly.

"Yes, no matter what that means." Bee got up, and I did too.

"It was nice seeing you again, Ava." We left the tiny visiting room and filed out past the dispatcher behind her desk. A few officers passed us by and greeted, either with a smile or nod.

Outside, we stopped next to the food truck, and I

rooted around in my handbag looking for my keys. "What do you think?" I asked.

"I think maybe Ava did it after all. Did you see the way she was talking about him? She was practically emotionless. She didn't seem to care at all."

"Then why did she cry at the beginning of this week?" I asked.

"I don't know." Bee tapped the end of her nose. "But we can't go back to the butchery without getting in trouble. I bet Detective Martin has his ear to the ground, and if he warned Clayton about us..."

"Right. So what do we do?"

"The only thing we can do," Bee replied, trying for a smile. "Decorate for Christmas. Maybe one of the committee members will know something."

Eighteen

THREE DAYS HAD PASSED SINCE OUR VISIT TO Ava, and we'd found a good ol' fat nothing in that time. If not for Bee's fabulous baking in preparation for the Christmas party that evening, I would have been down-right depressed.

No one could be sad after tasting one of her personalized miniature Christmas cakes. Ripe and sugared cherries had been used in the cake, with a delicious and light vanilla frosting that dripped over the sides.

I feasted on one and admired the hard work that we'd all put in to get the town hall ready for the party that would start in a little over an hour. Most of the decorating committee had cleared out, including Jerry and Misty, who had stayed for as long as possible before heading off to get dressed for the event.

Now it was only me, snacking on Christmas cakes, Bee, who had decided there was too little mistletoe in the hall and more was needed, and Millie, who'd stopped by with armfuls of tinsel and the excuse that she needed some time away from Greta Gould.

Greta. Babcock.

The murder.

It didn't feel right. Ava had acted strangely when we'd visited her, yes, but did that mean she was guilty of the crime? Maybe not. But the cops—

"Hey, Ruby," Millie called, teetering on the top rung of a ladder, "would you mind giving me a hand, dear, if you're not too busy?"

Millie was such a lovely woman. She'd let her hair gray out naturally and had chosen a warm, wooly sweater for the party so she wouldn't have to go home and change.

"Of course," I said and shoved the last of the cake into my mouth. I gulped it down and headed over to help out. "What do you need?"

"That string of lights there, please."

I lifted it and fed it up to her, and she proceeded to hang it carefully above the doors, pegging it in place. The string of lights only brought my thoughts back to the murder.

"There, now, that's better. Doesn't it look festive?" Millie asked, clasping her hands together. "I'll tell you,

Ruby dear, this is one hundred times better than working at the paper."

"I thought you loved your job," I said and held the ladder as Millie descended, her sneakers clacking on every rung.

"I did, before Greta came in and ruined everything." Millie dusted off her palms. "The woman is a complete and total menace. She's decided we're going to start publishing gossip stories about everything related to the murder."

"Really?" I asked. "Did she mention anything about Clayton Babcock?"

"No," Millie said, "and I don't think she will, since she's apparently the one who funded his campaign to run for mayor. But she *has* been spreading other vicious rumors around."

Even though we would leave soon, I did hope none of them were about Bee or me. I cared what the people of Carmel Springs thought of us. And when we did go, I wanted to leave them with warmth and joy and delicious Christmas cake miniatures. Not bad memories or gossip.

"Well," Millie said, lowering her voice and glancing around at the beautifully decorated hall, complete with red table clothes and a DJ booth. "She's started a rumor that Ava was having an affair."

"What? But I thought that definitely wasn't true."

"It wasn't. At least, I think it wasn't. Greta seems so convinced."

"Why?" I asked.

"Apparently, she saw Ava at the Clover Pot Hotel with someone. But she won't say who it was," Millie whispered, leaning in. "And rumor has it, they've been meeting in secret spots all over town. That's what she says anyway, but I don't know if that's true."

"Secret spots? I didn't realize there were any secret spots for people to meet."

"Oh, sure there are," Millie said. "Jeremy and Tilly were meeting out in the shed off Fifth Street. And when the Lobster Shack was closed, Henrietta sure sneaked in there a lot. And then there's the churchyard where—what? You've gone all wide-eyed."

"Did you say the churchyard?" I asked.

"Yes. It's right across the street. It's usually locked up tight, but I know for a fact that Juicy Jameson used to hang out there with his girlfriend. Before the winter." Millie shrugged. "There are all kinds of places people can meet, but I don't know if I necessarily believe what Greta's saying is true, dear. She's hardly the most trustworthy of sources." Millie patted me on the shoulder and hurried off to fetch more tinsel.

Bee had disappeared, likely gone to the bathroom. I

considered going after her, but this would only take a second. Assuming my hunch was correct.

Brick dust.

The churchyard.

Someone trying to keep us out.

My pulse pattered along at a furious pace. I sucked in breaths to calm myself. I had to go now. The party was due to start soon. The guests would be arriving. This was my chance!

THE SUN HAD ONLY JUST SET AS I CROSSED THE road, walking briskly, the cold wind whipping against my cheeks. I adjusted my fluffy earmuffs and my scarf and looked both ways down the street. The coast was clear, relatively speaking.

There were still folks moseying in and out of the Corner Café across from the town hall, but it didn't seem like anyone was paying particular attention to me.

The Christmas tree's festive lights were reflected in the windows of the buildings either side of Main Street, flashing merrily, and the distant singing of carolers drifted through the air.

"Quickly," I whispered to myself.

I closed my gloved hands around the gate's rungs and

hoisted myself over with lots of heaving and scrambling and the odd grunt. I landed on the other side, and my insides went all topsy-turvy. There were two fresh sets of tracks leading from the wall and back to the church. It was as if it hadn't snowed at all since we'd last been here.

Except I knew it had.

Lovers meeting in the churchyard? That had to be some type of blasphemy, especially since it might have been an affair.

But who was the mystery guy? And why was there brick dust on the snow again?

Brick dust!

Where did brick dust come from? Why from bricks, of course. And the entire church wall, barring the wrought iron spikes atop it, was made of bricks. I walked over to it, near where the footprints ended, my boots crunching on the snow.

I scanned the wall in the fading light then drew my gloved fingers across it. One of the bricks was loose and wobbled under my touch. Carefully, I slid it free and placed it on top of the wall. I bent and peered into the gap it had made.

There was something in there!

A letter?

I drew it out, quickly, brushed the dust off it and unfolded the page.

To my dearest Ava,

I hope that you'll get this letter before things go wrong. I know that you're probably unhappy about what happened, but you have to know that it was for the best. I needed to get him out of the way. He didn't treat you right.

You're the only one I can trust. I want you to know that I did it for you and for us. Once this all blows over, you and I can be together for real. In public.

Forever yours,

Jerry

Jerry? Jerry Flagg? The mayor's assistant?

I swayed on the spot, grasping the letter. Of course! Jerry had been there the day Ava had moved into the Oceanside. He had also been keen to help with the decoration of the hall, and he'd shifted blame toward Clayton Babcock.

I'd just found the final and likely only piece of evidence that proved Jerry was the murderer.

Nineteen

"Please," I said, as I strode back toward the town hall, "you have to come, detective. I have a crucial piece of evidence to give you that proves that it wasn't Ava who committed the murder."

Martin took a deep breath on the other end of the line. "You're sure about this? I have work to do tonight."

I frowned. Both Sam and Detective Martin had been invited to the Christmas party. Sam was most definitely coming, and I'd hoped Martin would too. We hadn't been the best of friends, but he had still been a part of our journey in Carmel Springs.

"Trust me, detective. It's worth it. I know who the real murderer is, and I am not kidding around."

"All right. I'll be there in fifteen," he said and hung up.

I hadn't even had the chance to tell him who the murderer was, but that was fine. Now I could only hope that Jerry would attend and wouldn't suspect anything. He surely hadn't been in the churchyard. I hadn't seen him there, at least.

By the time I entered the hall, the DJ had already started playing music—Michael Bublé of course—and people danced on the floor or ate food from the magnificent buffet table that Shawn and Sam had helped us set up. Folks carried miniature Christmas cakes or chattered, holding glasses of bubbly.

It was all so festive and sweet and definitely marred by my discovery. I scanned the crowd for Bee, but she was nowhere.

Sam stood over by the buffet table. She wore her mousy brown hair in a high ponytail and a splash of bright red gloss on her lips. It was the most makeup I'd seen her in, and she was absolutely stunning. Radiant, actually. A changed woman in comparison to the shy person she'd been months ago, when we'd first arrived in town.

She waved me over. "There you are. Bee's just run out to look for you. She was sure you were in the bathroom."

"Oh, I had to run an errand. Do you know when Bee will be back? It's sort of important." I continued searching the crowds in case Jerry had arrived.

"No, I don't know. But I'm sure she'll be back once she checks the food truck."

I brought my cell out of the pocket of my jeans and unlocked the screen, just as "Have a Very Merry Christmas" started up over the speakers in the hall. I had two missed calls from Bee and a text. I shot one off to her myself, telling her I was in the hall and had important news.

Then, I peered around again.

It was beautifully decorated now, truly festive with a Christmas tree either side of the stage, the tables clothed in red, and the mistletoe hanging from the ceiling. White lights flickered against the walls, and tinsel was strung up everywhere, looped perfectly by Millie's willing and able hand.

The song cut off, and the DJ tapped on a microphone on stage. "This great evening is all thanks to Bee and Ruby. Let's hear from 'em." Applause rang out, and my cheeks turned about as red as Sam's lip gloss.

I waved a hand in an effort to divert the attention, but the crowd was insistent. Oh, well, it couldn't hurt. Maybe I'd be able to spot Jerry from up on the stage. Or Bee. Or even Detective Martin. The letter in my pocket was practically burning to get out.

On the stage, I fiddled with the microphone, blushing furiously. I was so not good at being in the spotlight. That came with the whole debacle from my past and Daniel. *Definitely not the best time to focus on that, good heavens.*

I cleared my throat into the microphone, and it gave a shriek. "Sorry," I called. "Sorry. And hello, everyone. It's so good to see you all here." I scanned the crowd. Still no Jerry. But there was Bee! She waved at me and squeezed between the partygoers, heading for the stage. I smiled at her. "We want to wish everyone here a very Merry Christmas."

"Merry Christmas," everyone called, laughing and clapping. There were smiles all around. Except for Bee, who had stopped dead in her tracks, her eyes wide. She pointed at the stage, right at me, and shouted something that was lost in the noise. She waved, but I shook my head.

What was wrong?

Bee started shoving her way through the crowd, leaving a ripple of complaints in her wake.

"So, anyway. We wanted to thank you all for the most amazing few months we've ever had in this beautiful town. We've sold our cakes, we've had our fun, and we'll be moving on soon, but being here was an education in—"

An arm slipped around my throat and dragged me back from the microphone. For a hot second, I had no idea what on earth had happened, and I grappled with thin air. The smell of sandalwood eclipsed everything, and I peered up and found Jerry Flagg holding me tight to his chest.

"Hold still," he said, "or I'll kill you too. And your old friend."

"Old!" I choked.

Jerry didn't hear. He dragged me forward again, positioning himself in front of the microphone. "Hear me now. You will get the police to release Ava Jacobsen, and you will grant me immunity for the murder of Ian Jacobsen. If you don't meet my demands, the woman I have here will be collateral damage."

"Jerry, you don't have to do this," I said, grabbing at his hairy forearm. How could one man have so much hair? Oh wait, of course, it wasn't hair, it was his Christmas sweater.

"Shut up," he snarled.

My gaze swung wildly left and right, searching for help. I had called Detective Martin. Where was he?

I caught sight of Bee. She stood near the left Christmas tree next to the stage, a wicked gleam in her eye. She took hold of the tree and rocked it back and forth, back and forth. Jerry hadn't noticed. He was too busy professing Ava's innocence and his insistence on murdering me next. What a lovely Christmas this was turning out to be.

"—you will contact the head of the police, immediately," Jerry said.

I kept my focus on the rocking Christmas tree. I would have to pick my moment carefully. I had a black belt in karate, and I'd use it to my advantage the minute I was sure I had the upper hand. I had no idea whether Jerry had a weapon or not, but it was best not to risk it.

The Christmas tree crashed down against the side of the stage, bringing gasps and screams from the onlookers. Jerry's grip loosened a little.

Now!

I slammed my elbow into Jerry's solar plexus, drawing a pained growl. I stepped on his foot with the heel of my boot then spun out of his grasp and caught his arm. I twisted it behind his back and drove him down to the floor, placing myself atop him. "Got you," I said.

The crowd burst into screams and applause, and Bee rushed up to the stage. She helped me secure Jerry, his greasy ponytail flopping this way and that as he turned his head.

"Let go of me, let go!"

"I'm afraid not, Jerry," I said. "And Merry Christmas, by the way."

"Now there's a catchphrase you should keep." Bee nudged me with her elbow.

"It'll only work one time of the year."

"True, but imagine how confused people would be if you used it in July? Even better." The mirth in Bee's voice contradicted the concern in her eyes, but I still appreciated it.

A commotion broke out near the town hall's side doors, and Detective Martin appeared. He spotted us on the stage, and instead of groaning or scowling or frowning, he broke into a broad smile.

We'd done it again.

Carmel Springs was safe.

Twenty

Christmas morning had brought with it snow. We had a white Christmas, after all, the flakes pattering gently against the window. It wasn't too thick, but it was so cold that we'd gathered in the living room next to the crackling fire.

The stockings had been filled. Four in total.

One for Sam.

One for Shawn.

One for Bee.

And one for me.

Sam had also knitted a miniature sock for Trouble and filled it with kitty toys and treats.

The four of us warmed ourselves and sipped coffees and cocoas, grinning like we were kids on Christmas morning rather than grown adults.

"You really didn't have to get me anything," I said and reached into my stocking.

"Of course, we did," Sam said, grinning at Shawn. "We wanted to thank you for everything you two have done around here. Both at the Oceanside and in town. We're hoping if we butter you up enough, you'll come back next year."

"No butter required," Bee said, drawing a gift out of her stocking as well. "Unless it's butter on those delicious croissants Shawn made the other morning."

Shawn beamed at her. He was in another ugly Christmas sweater, still with the black kohl around his eyes, and now with a piercing in his lip. It didn't matter what he wore. Shawn had gone from troubled young man to responsible chef in the few months we'd known him. That made Christmas all the more sweet.

"Unwrap them," he said and dangled a bit of ribbon for Trouble to play with. The kitty cat leaped and turned, clawing and purring whenever he caught the end of the golden swatch of fabric.

I unwrapped my gift, and a soft piece of cloth fell out. I unfolded it and blinked. "This is too much, you guys. It's so nice."

"I've got one too."

Shawn and Sam had bought us matching aprons for

the truck. Both were covered in pastel pink and green stripes and had our names printed across the front.

"There's more," Shawn prompted.

We unwrapped a second set of gifts. Matching oven mitts. Bee and I both grew a bit watery-eyed. We gave Shawn and Sam a hug each then settled back to unwrap the last of our gifts.

Shawn had bought Sam a trophy that read "Best Boss Ever" as well as hand lotion because she'd complained constantly about how cold and dry her hands got during the winter.

Sam had bought Shawn a pair of stainless steel tongs, since he'd recently discovered a passion for barbequing and had started developing a rib sauce that was to die for. Hopefully, not literally.

Bee had gotten me a map, marked out with all the best tourist destinations we could visit, along with a notepad and pen to signify our investigations. On top of all of that, she'd gifted me a sterling silver pin that bore my name.

And I had gotten Bee a key chain with her name on it —since it was our long-standing joke that I could only drive and she could only bake—as well as a book she'd wanted all year: *Gennaro's Italian Bakery.*

Lastly, Bee and I had created Christmas cakes for Sam and Shawn, and Bee had written down her secret recipe for lemon meringue pie for Shawn to try out. It was a family recipe and one that she'd sworn she'd take to the grave.

"This is the best Christmas ever," I said, smiling at my friends. The friends I would so sorely miss once we had set off on our next adventure.

But that was life, wasn't it? There were beginnings and endings. Just because our time in Carmel Springs was nearing its end didn't mean we would never come back to visit.

"Wait until you taste the delicious meal Shawn's got prepared for lunch," Sam said, as Trouble leaped into her lap in search of comfort and maybe the shimmer of the trophy.

"I can't wait," I said.

"I'm already starved." Bee paged through her recipe book, pausing here and there to admire the pictures. "This is going to be a Christmas to remember."

TWO DAYS LATER, THE SNOW HAD CLEARED UP A little, the roads had been scraped clean, and we were ready to set off on our next big adventure.

Well, "ready" was a weighty term.

Tears gathered at the corners of my eyes as I hugged Millie on the steps of Oceanside Guesthouse's front porch.

"You take care now, dear. I'll send you emails and messages. And if you ever need anything, you know who to call." She patted me on the back.

Bee was already hugging Shawn. She'd struck up an unlikely friendship with him in our time here, and he seemed even sadder to see her go than she was to be leaving. "Now, young man," she said, "you keep doing what you're doing. You're going to be great, do you hear me? A great cook and baker. Your future is bright."

"Thanks, Bee," he said, choking it out.

I gave him a hug too then moved onto Sam and Trouble. "Please keep safe," Sam warbled, unable to keep her emotions in check. "And please call me. You've been such amazing guests and friends. And I just know little Trouble will miss you."

Indeed, the calico cat purred and licked me on the cheek the minute I lowered my face to give him a little kiss on the furry head.

"We'll be safe," I whispered. "And we will definitely keep in touch. Hopefully, we can swing back this way some time."

"You had better," Sam sobbed.

I hugged her tight, gave Trouble one final tickle behind the ears, then waved to my friends. My friends. Sheesh, I would never have thought that I'd have been leaving this small town in Maine with friends when I'd arrived.

I'd come to hide from my past. To find adventure. To explore.

I'd gotten so much more than that.

Bee and I walked arm-in-arm to the food truck, both overcome by emotion, holding the box of croissants that Shawn had given us. We got into the cab of the truck and took a second to compose ourselves. I afforded myself one last view of the Oceanside, with its two stories and the beautiful view of the ocean behind it.

Millie, Sam and Shawn waved from the porch, and I spared a last little goodbye for them, as well, then started the truck.

We drove off down the road, heading for the town's exit, my heart heavy.

"Cheer up, Rubes," Bee said. "We're off on our next escapade. Just imagine what the future holds."

"I know," I said. "I'm just going to miss them."

"At least we have the memories. Imagine if we'd never stopped in Carmel Springs. I'm sure we'll meet more fantastic people along the way."

"Hopefully, we won't have to solve any more murders."

"The world is full of wonder and strangeness," Bee said, turning to me with a gap-toothed smile. "I wouldn't count on a lack of mystery in our future."

I laughed, and some of the sorrow lifted. "So," I said, "where are we spending the New Year?"

"We're going to Muffin," she said, tapping on the GPS to bring up the map.

"Pardon me?"

"Pardon you," Bee replied. "Muffin, Massachusetts. I thought it sounded exactly like our kind of town."

I blinked. A chuckle burst from my lips. "All right," I said. "Muffin it is."

"Merry Christmas, Ruby. Let's have another adventure together."

"Merry Christmas," I said, my eyes on the road rather than the rearview mirror. "And a Happy New Year."

If you'd like to find out what happens in Muffin, Massachusetts, you can grab Murder Glazed Donuts at your favorite retailer.

If it's not in your local book store or library, be sure to request it from them!

Turn the page to read the first chapter!

Murder Glazed Donuts

CHAPTER 1

"ARE YOU TRYING TO CHOKE ME?" THE VOICE whip-snapped over the chattering crowd gathered in front of the food truck's open window.

I scanned the crowd, searching for the source of the disturbance, but no one stood out. Then again, it was pretty difficult to pick anyone out in the crowd. Bee and I had just arrived in Muffin, Massachusetts and set up our truck in front of the duck pond. Customers had swarmed in the minute we'd opened up 'shop,' and we hadn't stopped selling our special of the week since.

The strawberry glazed donuts were a bestseller.

"Did you hear that?" I asked my baking bestie, Bee.

"No. Hear what?" Bee had tied back her silver-gray hair today, and wore her signature Bite-sized Bakery apron, striped in pastel green and pink over a thick cream sweater.

She was halfway through a transaction, handing over a donut to a waiting customer. "Hear what, Ruby?"

"They're trying to choke me!" The voice came again. A woman speaking, for sure, but she didn't sound in distress. She was... angry.

A flash of red, followed by a few 'ows' and 'heys' caught my attention. An overweight woman in a turquoise tent of a dress, her hair dyed a shade of crimson that had come from a bottle, elbowed members of the crowd left and right. She stomped on feet, her blue eyes blazing hatred and locked onto me.

What on earth? What have I done?

"Bee," I said. "We've got a code red incoming."

"Excuse your pun," Bee replied.

Code red was our way of saying a dissatisfied customer was inbound. That or we'd just witnessed a fight, a murder, or walked in on a dead body. All occurrences that had been frequent during our time in Carmel Springs, Maine.

Oof, I have to stop thinking about that town. Ever since we'd left after Christmas, my heart had been trapped back in Maine. Which wasn't part of the plan—it was time to move on. That was the reason I'd gotten a food truck in the first place.

The redheaded firecracker reached the counter. She slapped a donut down onto it, smooshing crumbs and glaze everywhere. The customer in the line next to her flinched away, staring.

"Ma'am?"

"You're trying to choke me," the woman erupted, pointing a crimson fingernail at me. "You and your disgusting donuts."

"Excuse me, could you please lower your voice? You're upsetting the other customers," I said.

"Upsetting the other..." The woman's cheeks pinked. "Upsetting them? Who cares about them? What about me?"

"What's the problem?" Bee asked, always to the point. She didn't take kindly to being yelled, and she was protective of me.

"There's a fly in my donut," the woman said, pointing at the ruined treat. "Right there, see?"

I peered over at the flat counter and the crumbs spread across it. Pieces of the donut had been scattered everywhere, but there was no fly. I opened my mouth to tell her so, but that probably wouldn't go well.

And the other customers had started getting antsy. The last thing I needed was another repeat of our first weeks in the last town. We'd gotten involved in a murder, and that had changed the public's opinion of us at first.

A fly in the donut glaze wasn't as bad, but it was still a

reason not to visit the truck. I had to handle this perfectly. Diplomatically. I had to—

"There's no fly in that donut," Bee announced.

The woman glared. "How dare you. Are you calling me a liar?"

"That's exactly what I'm calling you."

The redhead gaped, her mouth opening and shutting. The other customers were just as round-eyed.

I patted the air in Bee's direction then turned back to the lady. "I'm sorry, what's your name?"

"Misty," she said. "Misty Murphy."

"It's nice to meet you, Miss Murphy. My name is Ruby and this is Bee. We're new to town. If there was a bug in your donut, I'd be happy to provide you with another one. Would that work for you? Free of charge?"

Misty gritted her teeth. "No. I don't want your disgusting donuts. You're horrible bakers. Your donuts are stale, anyway."

"That's not true," Bee growled. "We baked them fresh this morning. You're—"

"Bee." I had to keep things calm. It wasn't easy—the words had brought an angry boil in my veins. "Miss Murphy, I'd like to—"

"Save your breath." Misty shoved her hand toward me. "You've got nothing interesting to say." She stormed off, her red hair glinting in the watery sunlight.

A silence followed her departure. Then the gossiping started.

I pinched the bridge of my nose, forcing myself to take deep breaths.

"What a horrendous person," Bee said, and accepted money from the customer in front of her.

She wasn't wrong, but there was no use crying over... spilled donut?

"I'd better clean up this mess." I hurried past Bee and out of the truck. What a terrible start to our first day in Muffin. I'd hoped the friendly name of the town would carry over to the attitude of the locals.

I made quick work of dusting off the counter, apologizing to the customers lining up next to me.

One of them, a young woman with sparkling blue eyes like two gems in her pale face, greeted me with a warm smile. She was pretty enough to be a model, her golden hair in a bun atop her head. "Hello," she said, stepping out of the line and touching my arm.

"Hi. May I help you with something?"

"Oh, no, no, I'll join the line again for a cupcake, but I just wanted to talk to you about Misty."

"Misty?" I asked. "What about her?"

"Well, I wanted you to know that you shouldn't take her terrible behavior seriously," the blonde woman said. "Most of the people in Muffin don't really like her. And I know that's a terrible thing to say, but after what she said to you, I just wanted you to understand that no one takes her seriously."

"Oh," I said. "Oh, all right." I wasn't quite sure what to say. But I was definitely intrigued. *This is not another case to investigate, Holmes. Keep it together.* "Thanks for trying to set me at ease," I said. "I'm Ruby by the way." I brushed off my hand and presented it.

"Harper Kelly." She tugged on her ear, shyly. Her fingers were splotched with what looked like blue and yellow paint. "It's lovely to meet you and to have baked goods in town. We've had a serious lack of anything sweet like this lately."

"Why's that?" I asked, stepping away from the truck so that the other customers could file in and place their orders with Bee.

"Well, because of Misty," Harper said. "She owns the local bakery, but she's truly terrible at baking. No one wants to go there anymore. The Honey Bun in the center of town? Yeah, it's in the perfect spot to bring in business but... I had a donut from there the other day, and it had mold growing on it. Swore I'd never go back."

Eugh. That explained why Misty had thrown a full-blown adult tantrum about our donuts.

Harper shook her head. "People are saying Misty's dangerous—her father is the mayor—but I don't believe that for a second. She's just a sour woman who can't get her way."

"It sounds like she's gotten to you."

"Oh, she's gotten to everyone. Never has a nice thing to say." Harper tittered a laugh. "But what can we do?" She sighed. "We're stuck with her. I only hope that no one gets food poisoning from her bakery. I wouldn't want anyone to get hurt."

The information was a lot to process. I looked around, but Misty Murphy was long gone. "Can I get you something to eat?" I asked. "A cupcake, you said? No mold, I promise."

"That would be lovely," Harper said, rewarding me with another sugary smile.

Muffin already wasn't what I'd expected or hoped for. I got the feeling that things were going to be just as interesting here as they'd been in Carmel Springs. Was that a good or a bad thing?

Heavens, only time would tell.

If you'd like to find out what happens in Muffin, Massachusetts. Murder Glazed Donuts is available now. Head to your favorite retailer to get it!

More for you...

Sign up to my mailing list and receive updates on future releases, as well as **FREE** copies of *The Hawaiian Burger Murder* and *The Fully Loaded Burger Murder.*

They are *s*hort cozy mystery featuring characters from *the Burger Bar Mystery* series.

Head over to rosiebooks.shop to sign up!

Craving More Cozy Mystery?

If you had fun with Ruby and Bee, you'll want to meet Sunny and her Aunt Rita's cat, Bodger. You can read the first chapter of Sunny's story below!

The cat was out to get me.

It sat on the top step of my auntie's cottage, its black paws placed neatly beside each other, its yellow eyes focused on me. Every time I tried taking a step up the front path, it would hiss, fur standing on end.

Now, I hadn't exactly been expecting a welcome wagon when I'd arrived in Parfait, Florida, at the crack of dawn, but this was ridiculous. An angry cat, humidity that had no right to exist at 5:00 a.m., and the depressing realization that all my belongings fit into one wheeled suitcase —boy, was I living the life.

I cleared my throat, and the cat flicked its tail.

Why had Aunt Rita never told me she owned a cat? Though, in this case, it seemed more like the cat was the one who did the owning.

"Auntie," I warbled. "I'm here!"

She'd expected me two days ago, but paying my ex-husband's debts had taken longer than I'd hoped. There had been complications. People who I hadn't even known had had dealings with Damon had come out of the wood-work, looking for handouts. A lot of them were Russian. And intimidating. And had told me if I called the cops, I would regret it.

Try not to get depressed this early in the morning.

"Auntie Rita?" I called.

The cat hissed at me again.

"Oh relax," I said to it, hoping that my shouting hadn't woken the neighbors. Parfait was a small, coastal town, and the last thing I wanted was to make enemies on arrival. According to Aunt Rita, the locals adored her café and were pretty laid back, unless you got on their bad side.

I took a breath and fiddled with the extended handle of my suitcase. This was absurd. I couldn't let a cat get in my way. Aunt Rita had invited me to stay at her house while I got back on my feet after the messiest, scariest divorce in history.

And, yeah, I had been through the wringer, but I

wasn't about to let a feline with an attitude problem prevent me from having a good start to my "revival."

Granted, my revival had so far comprised three sweaty bus rides and being hit on by a toothless man who smelled of bourbon and peanut butter. Interesting combination, I'd give him that.

"Aunt Rita." I tried one last time.

The cat meowed, showing off disastrously sharp fangs.

"Look," I said, directing myself to the cat, "I like cats. Pretty much every animal is great in my books, barring chickens. Long story." I waved a hand. "The bottom line is, I'm expected, OK? Aunt Rita knows I'm coming, so you can chill out."

Another disdainful flick of the tail.

Grow a pair of ovaries, Sunny, for heaven's sake. What's the worst that could happen? It launches at your ankles?

I *did* have tender ankles.

"OK," I said, "I'm coming up."

The cat had understood that, it seemed, because it rose on all fours and yowled like a bat out of the nether. It hissed and spat, clawing as I walked up the cute path that led to Aunt Rita's single-story cottage.

"Shoo!" I waved a hand. "Shoo!"

The cat streaked toward me, and I braced for clawed impact. It disappeared underneath a bush rather than inflicting flesh wounds.

"Huh, would you look at that," I murmured. "All hiss and no claws." I trudged up the front steps, grinning at my silly idiom, and stopped on the cutesy, floral-print welcome mat.

I rapped my knuckles on the front door. "Aunt Rita?" It was early, but my aunt usually rose with the birds. She had when I'd lived with her, and I doubted that habit had changed over the last twenty years. Shoot, every Christmas I visited she'd wake me up with coffee at 4:30 a.m..

Twenty years. Gosh, was I really *that* old?

Thirty-eight and back at Auntie's house, looking for a place to stay, broke as the day I left.

I knocked. "It's me, Sunny." Still no answer.

The house was quiet as the grave.

Uh oh. OK, no need to panic.

My aunt always kept a spare key in plain sight in case she wasn't home when I came to visit. She'd changed her hiding spot from under the mat to the potted plant hanging from the eaves about a year ago. That was after I'd pointed out that everyone kept their spare key under the welcome mat.

I dug around in the soil in the potted plant and extracted the key. I dusted it off, my nerves building.

Why wasn't she answering the door? And why was her cat acting so weird? And when on earth had she gotten a cat?

I let myself into the cottage's entrance hall. It smelled faintly of lavender and chocolate chip cookies, as it always did. The evil cat streaked past me into the house, hissing for good measure, and I shut the door.

"Auntie?" I called out and flicked on the lights.

The place was immaculate—polished wood floors, styled in teal and cream, with framed pictures of me and Aunt Rita along the walls, showing my progression from geeky teenager to woman.

"Where is she?" I scooted my bag into place next to an end table. My gaze landed on an envelope propped against a vase of flowers. My name was scrawled across the front in my aunt's looping handwriting.

I lifted it, frowning. Why would she leave me a letter and not call me if she had a reason for not being here? Then again, I was a few days late.

I slit the envelope open with my aunt's silver letter opener and slipped out a single sheet of folded parchment paper.

My heart tha-thumped in my chest.

Dear Darling Sunny,

If you're reading this letter, I'm long gone. I regret to inform you that I've decided to go on a cruise with a few lady friends. To the Bahamas! Can you imagine it? Me in the Bahamas, sipping Bahamian drinks and dipping my toes in the water.

Now, you might think I'm crazy for leaving Florida, which is basically a prime vacation destination, but I need a break.

It's for this reason that I'm leaving you in charge of the Sunny Side Up Café until I get back.

I nearly dropped the letter in shock. "What?" I had no experience running a business whatsoever. I had gone to college to get a business degree, but my studies had been cut short when I'd married Damon. Besides, I couldn't cook a meal to save my life! Except for maybe spaghetti, and even that was touch and go.

I straightened the page and kept reading.

Don't worry, dear, you'll have plenty of help. Just try not to burn the place down while I'm gone.

I'll be unreachable for a few days until we've settled in, at which point you'll be able to contact me via the number on the back of this letter.

Have fun! Live a little!

Sincerely,

Aunt Rita

P.S. I've already had my neighbors feeding Bodger, but if you could take over from them once you arrive, that would be perfect. Also, Bodger hates everyone except for me, so make sure to lock your bedroom door at night. He has a tendency to leap at people's faces when they close their eyes.

Each word in the letter was worse than the last.

I was alone in my aunt's house with a homicidal cat and a café to run. Talk about out of my depth. And what had she meant about having plenty of help?

A knock rattled the front door, and I jumped and nearly dropped the letter.

Want to read more? You can grab **the first book, MURDER OVER EASY,** on every major retailer!

9 781776 432349